HUMAN CROSSINGS

9 stories about refugees

Foreword

Before the 21st century, the human tragedy of forced migration could be comfortably ignored for most of the time by those of us living settled lives in the West. Now, with a refugee crisis unparalleled since the Second World War, we have been forced to face up not only to the arrival in Europe of thousands of refugees from Asia, Africa, and the Middle East, but also to the reasons for these events. Among the many causes of the catastrophe in Syria, we cannot ignore the steady influx of refugees after the invasion of Iraq, and a series of droughts linked to climate change. War and famine have complex causes which are not restricted to the countries where they happen; it is not enough to put the blame on corrupt governments or tribal conflict. Knowing this gives us a sense of responsibility which can replace our helplessness.

The story of a refugee is usually like a long drawn-out nightmare. It involves the loss of home and family, of town or village, being denied a decent place to live in a neighbouring country, travelling long distances in depleted health, and, with luck, having to start again in a completely alien country. Nevertheless, many refugees have started again with cheerfulness and courage, putting aside fear and mistrust. Like soldiers after a war, refugees can only tell their story with painful difficulty. But those who have managed to piece it together can present us with a viewpoint which enlivens the grim news we have become weary of reading in the media.

Imagining the story, imagining the lives of others, is what these writers have set themselves to do. By inhabiting their characters they crystallise the massive problem of the refugee crisis into the microcosm of individual lives; so we see not just the trauma of displacement and danger but also the ordinary hopes, fears and loves experienced by any human being. By writing, by exercising their creative powers with the pen, writers can take responsibility. As I write this, an international Arms Fair is once again taking place in London. But the pen, if wielded with humanity and understanding, can be mightier than the sword.

Stephen Terry

Introduction

At the time this book was conceived in October 2017, the world was shocked by the photograph of the three year old Syrian-Kurdish boy Aylan Kurdi washed up on the shores of Turkey while crossing in a flimsy inflatable boat to Greece. The image of the boy lying face down on the sand symbolised the deathly plight of innocent refugees seeking refuge and safe haven in Europe. From that moment, things changed. Many European volunteers flew out to Greece to help welcome the hundreds of refugees risking their lives to cross the Mediterranean; donations flooded in; and a rise in awareness was tangible. The media began to take a more balanced and compassionate view of what they had dubbed the 'refugee crisis'. Politically, however, the refugee crisis continued to influence the right-wing resurgence across Europe. In the UK this led to Brexit, Britain's exiting from the European Union largely because of disgruntlement against migration.

This book is born out of a desire of eight authors to offer a more human and authentic depiction of what it means to be a refugee. Our intention is to shed light on the humanity of refugees and their right to live anywhere in the world. It is an attempt to present a counter-narrative to the media's bias, by suspending judgement and imagining the world of refugees: what motivates them to leave their lives and homes? Where do they find the inner strength to risk their lives crossing? What is it about the human spirit that thrives on hopes and dreams?

Each author has approached their aspiration for the book from a different and personalised angle. All eight authors are part of the Writers Empowerment Club – a wider group of 25 authors with writing ambitions – who support each other weekly on a group call. The Club was set up in May 2015, inspired by a number of aspiring writers on Landmark Worldwide's Team, Management and Leadership Programme in London. In October 2017, a small group from the Writers Empowerment Club were inspired to undertake a joint project. Dean Robinson, one of the authors, has experience in creative writing. He convinced the others to try their hand at it. We decided to embark on our own creative writing journey but we needed a focus – a shared theme where we could explore our self-expression. The refugee crisis captured our imagination. Some of the authors had first-hand experience visiting Calais and mentoring unaccompanied refugees, while others worked or socialised with refugees, and others felt compelled to learn more about the refugee crisis.

Photos of a visit to The Jungle before it was demolished (Credit: Noha Nasser)

We debated what title we would choose for the book and eventually settled on 'Human Crossings' as it possessed two important words for us. 'Human' is our anchoring of the stories in human experiences. Each author expresses themselves through the eyes, feelings, emotions and circumstances that migrants live as they traverse land and sea seeking refuge. The second word 'Crossings' represents the displacement of refugees geographically and psychologically from one place they called home to a new home – whether temporary or permanent. In the act of crossing is a sense of loss and leaving something familiar behind, while at the same time a sense of apprehension as they venture into an unknown future. These are major adjustments and require adaptation and courage to overcome. In writing our stories we have explored the motivations of migration, the dangers that sharpen survival instincts, and the ultimate humanity we all share. Through our journey of collaboration as a group of writers, we have made our own crossings into creative writing. The journey will lead us to donating fifty percent of all proceeds from the book sale to charities working for refugees.

The Auberge des Migrants in Calais December 2017 (Credit: Noha Nasser)

To immerse ourselves in the theme, we initiated a number of opportunities to learn more about refugees. In December 2017 Doug, Brigitte Deneck and Noha drove from the UK to Calais to visit the Auberge des Migrants on the outskirts of Calais. It is a warehouse co-ordinating the relief work for the refugees living in and around Calais. The Auberge has been the primary source of welfare for the Calais Jungle - the make-shift refugee camp that sprung up on the outskirts of Calais. A hub of volunteers work tirelessly to ensure refugees are fed, clothed, entertained and their mental health needs met. Now that the Jungle has been demolished by French Authorities in October 2016, the volunteers still continue their work, as Calais remains an important crossing point to the UK. While at the Auberge, Doug, Noha and Brigitte experienced the scale of the operation. Clothes were piled high in the warehouse. The kitchen was abuzz with large amounts of food being cooked. They interviewed a few volunteers to learn more about the refugees' living conditions and their interactions with them.

Brigitte D, Noha and Doug's trip to Auberge des Migrants in Calais December 2017 (Credit: Noha Nasser)

Later that month, Doug, Brigitte Deneck and Noha attended a play entitled 'The Jungle' at the Young Vic theatre in London; an immersive play winning five-star reviews. The stage was laid out as a series of narrow decks criss-crossing the theatre, with actors always in close proximity to the audience. The experience was overwhelmingly emotional and the script showed how the challenges of co-existence between nationalities in the Jungle created tensions over scarce resources. At the same time, threats from the French Authorities forced the same groups to seek solidarity and self-organise. Doug, Brigitte Deneck and Noha also learned about the tenacity of the human spirit; the hope, determination and resilience that the refugees possessed in their willingness to cross over to the UK.

Author writing retreats and meetings happened throughout the project (Credit: Noha Nasser)

At the same time, Ai Wei Wei's documentary film 'Human Flow' was released in London. Noha and Brigitte Deneck, with another Writers Empowerment Club author, Elston, met up to watch the film. 'Human Flow' is a powerful visual expression of the crossings of 65 million people in 23 countries seeking safety, shelter and justice. The documentary is extremely emotional as it records in real time the dangers refugees face crossing the Mediterranean, rivers, mountains and deserts. It also shows the shockingly cruel treatment of refugees as they arrive in some countries.

In December 2018, a group of us decided we needed to go on a writers' retreat to complete our writing project. Doug kindly invited us to his home in Devon. A few months earlier, he had met Khaled Wakkaa, a Syrian refugee living in Exeter. Doug was inspired by him and invited him to join us on the retreat. We spent the

whole day with Khaled and heard about the hardship he experienced leaving Syria, living in Lebanon and finally starting a new life in the UK with his family. It seemed that Khaled's story had to be in our book. Khaled embarked on writing his story in Arabic with the intention of having it translated. A second writers' retreat was organised in February 2019 in Southend-on-Sea and London with the aim of reading and editing the completed manuscripts.

The first story, 'Khaled's Story', is non-fiction. It is written by Khaled Wakkaa, a Syrian refugee, based on his personal experience crossing from Syria, to Lebanon and finally to Exeter in the UK. Re-telling events of his human crossing, Khaled encapsulates the determination and resilience of a refugee. Overcoming life-threatening situations, he eventually finds a way to safety in the UK through incredible synchronicities. Khaled also demonstrates how refugees can integrate quickly in their new home by volunteering and using skills and resourcefulness to reach out to others in society.

The second story, One+One=One, written by Brigitte Deneck is inspired by an Afghan refugee lodging in her home in London. Her story is one of friendship and love between two young boys. Their crossings together strengthen their bond to the extent they make a pact that if one dies the other will continue.

Noha Nasser is the author of the fictional story 'Amina's Diary: A Journey Crossing the Walls to Human Unity'. Noha visited the Calais Jungle a number of times and witnessed first-hand, through her assistance with psychologists and unaccompanied refugees, the determination and hope that seems to drive them to want to risk their lives. Transferring these ideas into a political context, Noha charts the travels of a young Muslim woman across different territories that challenge her identity in some way. Amina learns to love herself and her perpetrators regardless. Amina and Diane's character, Rubina, cross paths in their stories.

Diane Hands wrote the story 'Rubina's Story: Riches to Rags to Riches'. Diane sheds light on how skilled many of the refugees coming to Europe are, contrary to widespread belief. Her character, Rubina, is travelling with her father, an established doctor in Syria. The family endure much hardship as they make the crossing, in stark contrast to how they lived back in Syria. Diane describes how young Rubina takes on responsibility for her family after the loss of her mother, supporting her father and younger brother and sister with love and encouragement. Rubina, and Amina meet up in the Idomeni Refugee Camp in North Greece and a deep sisterhood is created.

'Holding On' is a fictional story by Dean Robinson. The main character Khalif experiences shipwreck in the Mediterranean, a common occurrence throughout the refugee crisis. Dean shows the wasted lives that many refugees experience as they face death. Khalif lived a normal life with meaningful relationships and deep bonds. Dean shows how in moments 'normality' is threatened, as is life itself.

Clara olde Heuvel, a Dutch immigration lawyer, is the author of 'A Treasure'. The story is largely fictional, although Clara has based part of the storyline on her encounters with a refugee whom she met while working as a legal advisor. The story is about Obabu, a Nigerian refugee who experiences deception, poor treatment, discrimination and bodily harm at the hands of bullies as he struggles to get to Europe. Once he makes it to Europe, Clara shows how through his continued hard work Obabu demonstrates to society that he has a valuable contribution to make.

'One Love' by Brigitte Fitschen is based on her autobiographical experiences with three partners from Eritrea, Nigeria and Congo who were refugees. Brigitte shows the plight of her main character, Finn, who has to use every resource he possesses to survive in Europe, including his body. Discriminated against in his own culture for being a homosexual, Finn has to find creative ways to make Europe his home including marrying a local lady who shows him love and compassion.

The last two stories are written by Doug Dunn. 'Crossing From India' is based on Doug's parents' emigration from India to the UK when he was a young child. He explores what it was like for his parents who were considered Anglo-Indians, a small community of migrating Indians who had mixed parentage. In writing this story, Doug set out on his own journey to find out more about Anglo-Indians and about his family history. He explores the themes of belonging and mixed-race identity in the UK.

'The New Jungle Project' is inspired by Doug's fascination with space. He creates a scenario where humans choose to find a new home on the Moon. Doug imagines how this might happen using material from 'The Jungle' show. His core message is that the new settlement on the Moon would be a world free of borders and discrimination. All would be welcome and equal.

This book is dedicated to all those refugees past and present, alive and not, who risked their lives to seek refuge and safe haven.

Noha Nasser

Khaled Wakkaa

I am 31 years old, from Syria. Because of the civil war I had to leave my country and go to Lebanon. I lived there with my new wife Dalal for several years, and we had a very difficult time. In March 2017 we came to England. We now live in a nice flat in Exeter, Devon, with our two daughters Lemar (aged 4) and Mila Prudence (aged 1). We have a happy settled life and are gradually improving our English; I am involved in lots of voluntary work and social activities. When I was asked to contribute my story, I knew that there was a lot to say and much of it was very emotional: so I decided to write it in Arabic, as I can express myself more freely in my native language.

Khaled's Story

Translated by Dr Alaa Nasser and Stephen Terry

Khaled offering free food and coffee in Exeter, UK (Photo credit: Khaled Wakkaa)

Syria

I will begin my story in 2011. I was at university doing a course in History. Like any other young man, I dreamed simple dreams and expected that life in my beautiful land of Syria would continue unchanged, with order and security prevailing.

But that year the war began. My university became a detention camp and I could no longer attend classes. Bullets and blood were all around me.

I had no work, nothing to study. It was dangerous to go outside. I had to hide. I couldn't see my friends. I became depressed, sleeping during the daytime and waking in the night to contact my friends via social media. Like this, I built up a little community of friends to share the agony and the brief moments of happiness. We became attached to each other. We made new friends, though the names we gave were false ones. But I believed every word that was said or written.

Meeting my life partner

Through the online programme MIG33 I was introduced to the girl who was to become my life partner. Her name was Dalal. Online, we told each other everything about our lives. Our relationship at the start was pure friendship, then it developed into a great love.

This went on for two years until I decided that I had to meet her. It was a very risky enterprise to travel across Syria in the middle of a civil war. But I knew that I had to reach this honest person who gave me such a feeling of security in this terrible time.

Dalal lived in Homs, in the southwest of the country, I lived in the northeast. I travelled south by bus, while fighting raged and military planes dropped bomb barrels. No one could predict when they would fall, or on whom.

Homs was being besieged by the Syrian army. It was impossible to enter, so I stayed on the outskirts. I managed to contact Dalal and waited till she found a way to get me into the city.

Eventually I reached a street near where she lived. But how would we recognise one another? I had to give her a description of my clothing and where I was standing. Moreover, it was much too dangerous for her to leave her house, particularly during the curfew. So she had to hire a car to reach me. The whole situation was horrifying.

When I saw her, everything around me dissolved. I forgot the time and the place. I lived moments stolen from time, beautiful moments.

Then I woke from my dream to the bitter reality that we were not free to walk around the streets because of the curfew. I needed a safe place to live, but it was impossible for Dalal to stay with me. So I found a room for a couple of days: it was shared with four other young men. Each night Dalal and I spoke on the phone till the crack of dawn, losing track of time.

Decision to escape

The next day we met, but outside was the reality of war: checkpoints prevented us from staying together for long. So we decided to go into a jewellery shop and buy rings: wearing them, we could talk more freely. I must explain that our traditions and the culture of Eastern society forbid a girl from talking to any man before marriage. Now the war had put us under even more pressure. There we were in the deserted streets, with nothing but the smell of death. Although this prevented us from experiencing the beautiful happiness of love, I put the rings on her hand, an action supposed to be done in the presence of both families at a formal party.

It was time for me to go. I left Dalal behind, but my heart was still connected to her. When I got back to my city the situation had become much worse, and I didn't know how I would ever see her again. My city was controlled by different armed groups. If I stayed any longer I would be forced to fight for one of them. So I decided to escape from Syria.

Getting married

I boarded a bus to Lebanon. As Homs was on my route, I got off the bus there. This time I was in Homs on official business: I was going to get engaged! Dalal had accepted me; now she was waiting for me. The only sadness was that my family would be absent. They accepted the situation and the fact that our two families would not meet.

We signed the marriage contract in the presence of the imam of the local mosque. Bombs were falling all round us. I don't know how to convey the scene to you. One bomb fell on a house only a few metres away, shattering our windows. Glass lay everywhere. We were all shocked by the massive force of the blast and the deafening noise, and we could see the planes overhead. We recited the Quran and prepared to meet death if that was our fate. Then we completed the formalities of our betrothal.

The next day I continued my journey to Lebanon. When I arrived, I went to the mountainous area of Bchamoun not far from Beirut. There I started looking for a simple job and a small place for us to live together. It took ten days to find a house, and every day seemed like a year. Then I went back to Homs for the wedding ceremony. There was no party, but Dalal's family and close friends were present. It was September 28th, 2013, a date I'll never forget, the day I married the girl I loved.

Bchamoun, Lebanon

A week later we were back in Lebanon, me with my passport, Dalal with her ID card, both tired from the journey, carrying just two dusty suitcases, the signs of our migration. We found our house. It was in a bit of a state, so I cleaned it till night fell.

Neighbours came and invited us to rest in their homes. But daily life was hard and the winter was cold. I took every job available - picking olives, doing painting, decorating and electrical work, even working as a barber. But none of this was enough to give me respect: I was a Syrian. Sometimes, my employers only gave me part of my wages. Sometimes they avoided paying me at all.

Another problem was that our landlord raised the rent. The house wasn't pleasant to live in anyway, as it didn't see any sunlight. So, as Dalal was now pregnant, we decided to move. We were starting from scratch again.

16

Some kind people originally from Syria but with Lebanese nationality gave us part of their garage. I managed to convert it into two rooms with a kitchen. We bought a TV and second-hand household items, and the family gave us a few things. Here at last we began to feel some stability and security. Peace entered into our lives, and soon there was the joyful arrival of our beautiful daughter. We named her Lemar.

Threatened with death

Almost immediately a fateful night came when I was arrested. About midnight a car drew up outside our house and I was bundled into it. I was taken to a place where I was beaten and insulted. When I asked what I had done wrong, they kept beating me. Eventually a man arrived who seemed to be the leader: he asked me why I had threatened to kill a certain Lebanese man, who they named. I was bewildered: I had never met this person. Now a woman appeared, telling me that if I didn't leave the area, my family and I would be killed.

I was in a state of shock. My body was broken by the beating and my mind was numb. I had no idea what to do and I felt completely powerless. I just wanted the earth to swallow me up so that I could disappear.

They threw me out on the doorstep of our house. Dalal was distraught, not knowing where I had been.

Another man turned up and warned us that we would be killed if we didn't leave immediately. He said we would be thrown into a wadi, or valley, below Mt Bchamoun. So we gathered up our clothes and left our warm home and everything else inside it. I'll never forget the fear on my wife's face, the woman I had promised to make so happy.

Afterwards I found out who these gangsters were. They belonged to the National Socialist Party which support the Syrian president Bashar Al-Assad. The woman was an informer who had also planted Isis flags in some other refugees' house to get them arrested.

We decided to go to Tripoli in northern Lebanon, because it would be safer there, being a Muslim area, not Druze. We had to go through Beirut, so we went to the UNHCR office to complain. We were given an appointment a few days later. So now we were on the streets, with my wife still breastfeeding our baby daughter. At night I held tiny Lemar in my arms, sheltering her from the cold air. When the day came for our appointment, we were full of hope. But our hopes were dashed. The UN official had no sympathy for us, despite the fact that Dalal was exhausted from nursing our baby daughter and lack of sleep. Instead of showing us kindness, the woman kicked us out saying, "Do you expect us to give you your own private security guard? Go and complain to the police."

It was little consolation to know that all Syrians were treated like this in Lebanon. Because of their reputation for always complaining, Syrians were regarded as liars.

Tripoli: living in a car-repair workshop

On the long bus journey north, Lemar was crying continually. You wouldn't believe how desperate we felt when we arrived. We just stood in the street with no idea what to do, or how to find a place to sleep. I pitied myself, I felt heart-broken for my wife and daughter.

After a time, an old man came up to me.

"I have a metalworking workshop," he said. "We use lathes to make and assemble car-parts. You can go and live there and arrange it for yourselves. It's better than the street."

The place stank of oil and diesel. At night we slept on the floor and we spent our days on the street. I found some work in a foundry doing 16 hours a day and returning with hands bleeding and bruised. Dalal was miserable and riddled with illness, and baby Lemar had a nasty rash caused by an allergy. When I went to the UN office in Tripoli the receptionist insulted me, calling me a liar, laughing and taunting me and saying that we were cursed by God. Even though we went to the UN day after day, standing in the queue from dawn to dusk, no one helped us. Most of my wages were spent getting home again by public transport.

One day while we were roaming the streets with Lemar on my shoulders, a man came up and asked if we needed milk, blankets and household items. "Yes we do," I said. The man said he was from a French charity which helped refugees. He wanted to see our home and to take copies of our papers. At last there seemed to be hope! It never occurred to me that he might be lying. In my happiness I forgot to ask him for his ID. He took our papers and returned a few days later, saying that if I didn't give him $75 he would hand us over to the Lebanese Intelligence Department because our papers showed that our right to stay in Lebanon had expired. We had to pay him several times; he knew that he was taking money needed to pay for food and medicine for my sick wife, but he didn't care. He wasn't a charity worker; he was an informant from a Sunni group. It seemed because we were Syrians, we would always be treated badly.

The hospital in Beirut

So after 45 days in Tripoli we hurriedly packed our bags and took the bus to Beirut. Here we found a room above a bakery in the Jnah district near the sea. It had a kitchen area and one end of it was partitioned as a bathroom. There was no sunlight or ventilation, and the heat coming up from the bakery was unbearable. So we soon left and found another room nearby. To have enough money for rent, Dalal and I had to take it in turns to eat. One day I had bread and water, the next day she did. Once we went without any food for four days. Dalal was down to 35 kilos: she could no longer breastfeed Lemar, so we bought milk. The landlady had no sympathy for Syrians: when she saw that Dalal was anaemic, she said, "Poverty is in your blood." One day some men came and wrote down our names and other details: they were planning to hand me over to Hizbollah, who were recruiting young men to fight for the army of the Syrian regime.

Meanwhile I was working as an electrician and any job I could find, even cleaning. One day I came back to the flat and found that Dalal had collapsed and fainted. I contacted the Red Cross who gave her oxygen and took her to A&E. I entrusted Lemar to a kind neighbour from Ethiopia, and went to the hospital.

Dalal's blood pressure was so low that she was about to go into a coma. Unless she was admitted to hospital, she wouldn't survive.

I now had two urgent problems: how was I to find money for my wife's treatment, and how was I to look after my young daughter? I remembered that I had the phone number of an elderly lady called Latifa Katooa, who was a friend of Dalal's mother and lived in Tripoli. She came over from Tripoli and took Lemar back to her home. I will be eternally grateful to her.

At the Al-Harriri hospital, the receptionist told me that as I couldn't pay the initial amount of $700, I would have to take my wife away. A doctor said that if I did that she would die. I was in tears. A woman from social services told me to go and ask for money from all the charities and organisations which help refugees. I took her advice, leaving Dalal in A&E, and going round to any charity I could find. The Islamic Dar Al-Fatwa gave me a kilo of dates: what good was that? Other organisations were equally unhelpful.

When I got back to A&E, Dalal was lying on a metal box in a store-room.

Fortunately the Head Doctor of the hospital, Dr Ghazi, promised to help us: he said that he would arrange for Dalal to be admitted if I could raise $200. With the help of some friends I produced this amount, and after two days of waiting Dalal was finally given a bed. It was ironical that this was the first night in two years of homelessness when we had a proper bed and could watch TV!

They did a bone-marrow autopsy and found that Dalal was malnourished and was deficient in vitamin B12 and calcium. She was being fed intravenously, but this soon stopped as we couldn't pay. Meals also stopped and the room wasn't cleaned because we were Syrian.

A benefactor

Someone advised me to put everything on Facebook. I did, and people responded with moral support. Then a man phoned offering to pay most of our expenses, saying he would come over in person. So I went to meet him at the accountant's office in the hospital. When I got there I saw through the glass partition someone being stopped by the Lebanese soldiers guarding the hospital; it was him. Apparently he wasn't legally resident in Lebanon. I felt guilty about his arrest.

I went outside to get some fresh air, and a call came through on my mobile phone. At that very moment a motorbike whizzed by, and my mobile was snatched from my grasp. I couldn't believe what was happening. I could only laugh and cry at the same time.

The pressure on us continued for the next two days. Doctors and nurses told us to go back to Syria. But they didn't dare to remove Dalal themselves because of her critical condition. Finally Dr Ghazi ordered the staff to resume treatment and give us our meals. We stayed in the hospital for ten days while Dalal regained her strength a little. Then our would-be benefactor phoned again and arranged to meet me in the street. This man, who was a Syrian refugee himself, had managed to raise a good deal of money through friends. He handed me the money and advised us to leave the next day.

On the streets

When we checked out, all the doctors and nurses clapped. I wondered why. Anyway, we were glad to have escaped from their grasp. We were keen to get back to our rented room.

There we found that the landlady had scattered our possessions all over the place. Dalal was furious, accusing her of stealing our valuables. The landlady laughed and sent for her son-in-law, who worked for Hizbollah. He started accusing us, took our papers and kicked us out.

We were on the street again.

There was no way we could have Lemar with us now. It was a moonlit night, and we raised our spirits by looking up at the sky and thanking God that we were alive and well. Dalal finally went to sleep with her head on my shoulder, and I stayed awake till sunrise.

21

A new day was born. We set off. Dalal was still weak and kept losing her balance. She put a mask over her mouth, fearing to pick up any diseases. Rather than feeling tired, I felt guilty for getting her into this state. And we were still without our daughter.

In the Hadas area we found the office of the Caritas society. A soldier tried to push Dalal away, saying we were liars. I was about to attack him, but Dalal told me to be patient. After vainly searching for other charities we went back to the Rosha area where we took it in turns to sleep.

Help at last

We had been told about an organisation called Basmeh & Zeitooneh (the name means "Smile and Olive"). This charity, set up to help Syrian refugees was in Lebanon, particularly in Beirut, and they work together with Médecins Sans Frontières. Their office was in Shatila, the part of Beirut with a large Palestinian camp. It was a dangerous area but Dalal was intent on going there.

On the door was a notice saying 'Protection Office'. Dalal told me to stay outside in case I got angry; she knew that she would be able to control herself. I waited outside. After a time she came out with a smile on her face: there was good news, she said. I felt a wave of relief. We went in together and I saw a room like a nursery, decorated with children's drawings, with a small library and a desk.

Behind the desk sat a woman called Niebal Al-Olw. She was a psychologist, though we didn't know that at the time. "I am here to help you," she said. Instead of doubting Dalal, she treated her humanely. She gave us money for a meal and asked the manager of Basmeh & Zeitooneh to pay a month's rent for a flat until I could find work. At the request of Niebal, the charity gave us bedding, kitchen utensils and furniture. The next day I went to fetch Lemar. I was starting to feel optimistic!

It seemed a good idea for Dalal to have some sessions with Niebal, so as to regain some energy and positive feelings. She told Niebal the details of everything that had happened to us. Niebal suggested that we put forward our story to a solicitor from the International Refugee Assistance Project (IRAP). We did this.

Working at UNICEF

We were also introduced to a lady called Adria Al-Hussein, who worked as a volunteer for the United Nations. She took us under her wing. She found me work in a restaurant and also at a UNICEF centre. I worked at the UNICEF centre from 9-5, and at the restaurant from 5-10 in the evening. This was quite tiring but I was glad to be working and earning money. Adria also sent Dalal meals every day and clothes for Lemar. Dalal has a university degree in Arabic literature, and Niebal found her a teaching job at the Basmeh & Zeitoonehschool. Meanwhile Lemar went to the charity's nursery.

A month went by and we had forgotten that we had sent our story to IRAP so it was a surprise when we were contacted by them. They were going to register us as refugees so that we could be resettled! We were full of joy and hope.

Problems in Shatila

But at this time there were many problems for us in the Shatila camp. The ground-floor room we had rented was in an isolated area without any neighbours, and at night we could hear the frightening noises of shooting and the cries of people being tortured and begging for help. We went to look at another room owned by a Palestinian woman. The room needed repairing and she demanded money for this. We handed over some money, but once she had it she threw us out, threatening to kill us. We knew the law of the camp: anyone could be killed, and no one would ask any questions. Eventually we found a room which felt a bit safer; it was in the same area, but on the second-floor.

We were attacked several times. One day Dalal was passing under a balcony and a big stone was thrown at her, injuring her head. She was in a lot of pain and her hearing was affected. At the clinic, the doctor wrote a false report, claiming that we had been quarrelling. Another time, while I was at work, a teenager threw a firework at Dalal. When I challenged him about it, he called all his friends and they attacked me with knives. My UNICEF friends defended me and the episode only came to an end when I apologised to the boys.

It didn't stop with that. I was carrying some equipment which the manager of the UNICEF centre had entrusted me with. Two men approached me; one took out a gun and put it to my head and kicked me. People gathered round to watch. The two men were gripping me and keeping the gun to my head. Eventually the manager came out with several staff members and wrestled them away. My attackers had wanted to humiliate me and show how strong they were. One of them was from the Palestinian mafia who sold drugs to children.

There was more trouble with our neighbours. They started to insult us and threaten us. They broke down our front door. One evening at 8 o'clock Dalal opened the door to a neighbour she didn't know. This woman started hitting and kicking her, saying that she hadn't helped her clean the stairs. Everyone knew that Dalal went out to work - but the cleaning couldn't be postponed till the weekend! The woman then threatened to send men to beat us up. I had to do something about this, so I went to the protection department of Basmeh & Zeitooneh and asked them to intervene. They tried to calm everyone down.

Leaving Lebanon

Now at last things were speeding up with our resettlement. We had several meetings with IRAP and with UNHCR. We were informed that the UK had officially accepted us and that arrangements were being made for us to be flown there, but first we would need a health check.

Only a few days remained before we would leave our 'house'. I will describe it to you. It consisted of a small room with a kitchen area and bathroom, and no windows. Water dripped through the ceiling constantly and we would wake up in the night to find ourselves drenched. All our bedding was wet with salty water. We bought bottled water for showers and cooking, so we thought that we were all right. But this water was poisoned! We spent a whole night taking serum injections so that we would pass the health check.

Finally the day came: it was March 28th. We were driven to Beirut airport at midnight. I remember the wonderful feeling I had when I entered the airport building. Beautiful thoughts of how my wife and I were going to live in security and dignity. It was a dream which we could hardly believe might come true. But that soon changed when we had to go through security and then wait two hours. Every minute felt like a year, as we feared that our emigration would be refused and we would be told to go back. But finally we boarded the plane and it took off. At 4 a.m. we arrived at Frankfurt, where we had to change planes.

Arrival in England

We landed at Bristol airport at midday on March 29th 2017. At last we had arrived in the UK! During the flight we had been so excited about our new life. At the exit gate I saw a man holding a placard with Arabic writing: it was my daughter's name, Lemar! Also there to meet us was Annette Hughes, the Head of Refugee Support Devon (RSD). She was a marvellous lady, full of understanding and with a wonderful spirit. Her warm welcome made us feel very happy.

We began the journey by car to Exeter, where a house had been made available for us by the British government. Unfortunately, we were also accompanied by a Syrian man who wanted to dominate us and control our lives. For the next two weeks he made himself a nuisance. Finally, with the help of RSD, we managed to get free of him. It is a pity that some Syrians do not want to integrate into life in the UK, but for me this is very important.

When we arrived at our flat, Annette gave me the keys and I passed them to Dalal. This was a special moment: we were entering our new home! The flat was totally different from the small dark room we had in Lebanon. It was spacious and light, up on the first floor, with a balcony on two sides and a lovely view of a play park, the river Exe with ducks and swans, and the Cathedral. Everything was new: in the kitchen we found a fridge, gas cooker, washing machine, toaster, microwave, cutlery, the lot! The bedrooms had bedding and many cupboards. There was plenty of room for Lemar to run about and play. For the first few days, we just sat indoors as if we were in a dream!

Our life in Exeter

A week after our arrival two English people called Hannah and Tristan, who I had got to know in Lebanon, came and visited us. How happy we were to see them again and also meet their friends. They helped us get to know the area near our flat, showed us the best shops, gave us useful contacts and told us where to go for help.

Someone else we had met in Lebanon was a lady called Prudence. She now became like a mother to us and a grandmother to our children. She has given us great emotional and practical support. When Dalal was pregnant she came with us to the ultrasound, and she attended the delivery. And when we knew the baby would be a girl we decided to name her Mila Prudence. We are so happy that Prudence is part of our life.

When we first arrived we spoke only a little English and we hardly knew anyone in Exeter. However, through Facebook I found out about a social event nearby, and after being given a warm welcome I invited these new friends back to our flat. This gave me the confidence to get involved in more local activities, and I joined a "Free Moovement" exercise group in the park, which I am now leading. I also take groups of people on cycling trips called "Freewheelin". Also through Facebook I made friends with someone called Zelah. Zelah has become like a sister to Dalal and me, encouraging us to be positive and integrate in the community.

I love working with children. In Lebanon I had gained a certificate in social work, so when Lemar started going to a nursery, I volunteered to help there, doing artwork with the children, and drumming. The very helpful manager of the nursery gave me a course in safeguarding.

26

Then I joined a group of volunteers who clean up public places. While doing that, I noticed a street stall, so I went and talked to the people: it was called "Food Fight", and I offered to cook some okra and rice and bring it the next time. I now cook for "Food Fight" about once a month, and I also offer free haircuts. My Syrian food is popular, and I am very happy to be giving hot meals to people, especially the homeless. As a refugee in Lebanon I was not treated kindly, but now I feel I am restoring humanity! I have recently done a course in food hygiene. I also volunteer at a cafe in a Baptist church, and have picked up some office skills by working at a reception in the busy Community Centre. Doing voluntary work has helped me improve my English a lot.

Through these activities I have made a lot of friends of different nationalities and religions. I think I have the ability to bring people together: it was my idea to hold a festival in this part of Exeter called 'St Thomas Together'. It is a kind of international celebration, and so far it has taken place twice, in summer 2018 and 2019. Lots of people have helped and contributed, and there is so much interest that we are planning to hold it in the winter too. I would like to build on my involvement with the local community and try to benefit the community as a whole: perhaps one day I will become Mayor of Exeter!

This is an amazing country. When I see my family warm and safe, I feel great satisfaction and I know that I am in the right place. I want to encourage all refugees to break out of their shells and try to integrate with life in the UK.

Recently I met Doug Dunn at a Landmark Forum event, and he invited me to write my story and contribute to a book. I hope that my story will be a message of encouragement to anyone who reads it.

Brigitte Deneck

I was born in Lille (France) and studied Politics at the Institut d'Etudes Politiques de Paris. When unrest erupted in 1968, I joined the editorial team in the occupied Higher Education institution and provided information on what was happening in universities and in French society as a whole. Later I produced street theatre which had the same purpose: to provide an insight into the events, help people understand and inquire.

Further theatre studies led me to the US and Poland, and I later specialised in a method of self-development through voice, which has been my main activity in the UK. I have translated from French a book about this method, Le Chant de l'Être (Song of Self) by Serge Wilfart.

Keen to inform and inspire further, I joined the Writers Empowerment Club created by Noha Nasser. When the idea of collective work came up involving writing short stories on the topic of refugees, I saw this as a way to help people grasp reality through fiction. My story is grounded in real stories of real people, and invites the readers to consider what they ultimately stand for.

One + One = One

(Photo credit: Brigitte Deneck)

Calais December 2017

"If I die, you continue."
"If I die, you continue."
Their fists touched briefly. The pact was sealed.

Through the cold damp air, Ahad and Wahid ran towards the place where some of their friends had already gathered for a game of cricket. All were talking and laughing, stepping backwards and forwards, dancing with excitement. It took a little while to bring the teams together and for each to choose the first two batsmen. Ahad and Wahid ended up in the same team. For three hours bowlers came and went. Everybody went crazy when the score tied at 70 for both teams. Super Over! They all forgot how exhausted they were and jumped in all directions, throwing themselves on the ground, shouting "Super Over! Super Over!" Each team huddled and started the negotiations to select the batsmen. Ahad was chosen. Ahad's team needed six runs to win. He stood facing the bowler. The bowler ran up, hurled the ball at Ahad and he hit it as hard as he could. The ball drew a perfect curve against the clouds. It seemed it would not end. They all gasped when the ball landed off the field. Six runs.

This time the boys in the winning team started laughing and crying, embracing each other. Flying towards each other as if gravity were suddenly lifted, they formed the epicentre of a whirlwind that moved in the direction of the sea, a swarm of birds evolving in different shapes against the background of sand, sea and sky.

Some stopped in their tracks. Standing on the cricket ground, Wahid remembered.

He had crossed waters to arrive here. He remembered the Mediterranean. Not the colourful sunny tourist-friendly beaches, but the waves that threatened to swallow rubber boats bursting with people of all ages.

Wahid remembered one of his worst moments on the journey. Walls of water around a rubber dinghy holding 56 people somewhere between Turkey and Greece. They had blown up the boat with two pumps from the box they had been given. One of the passengers had been instructed to steer it. Men, women, families and young boys like him had climbed on the boat. They were now screaming their prayers. The newly trained pilot asked Wahid to help with pouring fuel in the tank. Immediately the smell made him so sick he became unable to see and breathe among the spasms that shook his stomach. When Wahid opened his eyes again, he saw the shore: people, cars. Everybody around him was screaming with joy this time. He started praying.

Now there was another sea to cross. Why?

Why not stay in France, where they had been for months? Some were now considering it. The process for claiming asylum sounded slow. When asked, their hearts sank. What came up at once was the image of the 'CRS', the French crowd control police: masked policemen armed with batons to break bones, tear gas to choke you before you spoke, blades to rip tents, grenades to make holes in shelters.

From the cricket ground, Wahid followed those who walked towards the sea, their faces lit up in the afternoon light. They strode with their chests wide open, ready to jump into the unknown.

Standing on the sand, they looked beyond the blurred horizon where England lay, and repeated in an impatient tone: "When are we going to cross? When are we going to cross?" The soft breath of the sea kept flowing back and forth.

They returned inland, spreading over the beaches, dunes and wasteland. Wahid and Ahad stayed together. Wahid was 14 and Ahad 16. Wahid meant 'the One', a name for Allah, and Ahad meant 'the One' as well. Ahad had been in Calais longer. It was natural for him to help a fellow Afghan find his way. Ahad told Wahid everything about the ritual of the crossing. Repeatedly they climbed on lorries with the hope to cross through the tunnel to England. Repeatedly, they came back after pepper spray had forced them to leave the corner where they were hiding.

But Ahad had a new idea for tonight. Wahid's excitement grew. He thought of London. His brother Mukhtar looked so happy in the picture of Tower Bridge. Everything would be over soon.

"Meet near the roundabout at nine, OK?" said Ahad. He wanted to get something from the town and went one way. Wahid went the other way and reached the caravan. This was part of the complex around the 'Auberge des Migrants': a large warehouse where clothes were being sorted, a kitchen recently extended where volunteers were chopping vegetables for the evening meal to distribute in some spots around town, a van for public relations and information, another colourful van labelled 'school' and one caravan as an office. The office was managed by a British volunteer called

Rachel. She waved at him: "I have a message from your mother. She wants you to call.""OK... I am coming."

His mother's figure suddenly came to his mind, tall in the blue burka, and what was said on that day when she ordered him in a stern voice to go and be strong. His father had been killed by the Taliban because he worked for people they did not like. As the eldest son he could be next. Everything was arranged by his uncle. Then he started his journey.

Her voice at the other end trembled. "Yes Mum... Yes I am fine now. I have a nice room in the town of Calais. I have seen the legal adviser. The application is complete! So I can join Mukhtar! Yes! Yes!" The more he lied, the more assurance he found in adding details. His hands punctuated the lies with enthusiasm. "Yes Mum! Bye!"

For a moment, he remained still and started shivering. Rachel invited him to sit on the electric heater: "You can stay here for a bit, and then there will be dinner. What about a cup of tea?"

He felt good with Rachel. Sometimes she also gave them English lessons. Maths was taught by a funny Englishman with a long red beard called Chris. Yesterday's lesson had been incredible fun. Wahid had learned about mathematical paradoxes. What a laugh! Then he made up a problem, claiming that 1+1 = 1. Nobody could figure it out.

He said: "One flame added to one flame is one flame. One promise added to one promise is one promise". He left them to think, giggling as if it were the best joke he had produced in his whole life.

Next he was going to move his sleeping bag, which he had left a bit too exposed in the woods. Not many trees in these woods. He walked for about twenty minutes on the side of the road, then turned right and passed some meagre bushes and bare trees. He left the path to enter a more sheltered area. Two men had lit a fire. He stopped for a minute. They signalled something had happened, pointing in different directions. Wahid came closer, and then raised his head. He smelt the air, ran and turned, holding the sleeping bag with his foot, throwing it away from him. Again and again, he kicked it and finally left it behind. Tear gas - now it was impossible to use the sleeping bag. This was too much. He walked back, his head bent, mumbling and swearing. Anyway he was crossing today.

At nine o'clock Wahid stood near the roundabout and his friend appeared. Ahad took the lead, walking fast on the right side of the motorway.

Ahad kept marching on, then turned to see if Wahid was following.

Ahad saw a big lorry hit him, drag him along the side and thunder past. He fainted. He opened his eyes to the sound of sirens, saw flashing lights, and fainted again.

He was taken to hospital in the same ambulance as Wahid. Then he was dropped near the Auberge.

The next day, Ahad went to the mortuary and took a picture of Wahid, covered up to the neck with a white sheet. He remembered: "If I die, you continue". It was for him to carry the flame forward.

He took the money Wahid had left, resolved to use it well.

This time he found a smuggler who guaranteed a safe crossing. He paid him, knowing there was no guarantee but his faith. With about 40 others, he was led as far as a ditch which crossed their path. He measured the two to three metre wide trench and jumped first. His hands landed in a bush of thorns. A few others followed, until the police came to disperse those who were still hesitating.

Ahad ran and ran towards a lorry. He had never run so fast. He jumped on the lorry and hid in the furthest corner, behind plastic sheets that could crush him any time. Two others had managed to climb as well.

The lorry passed the police, the dogs, customs. It stopped on the ferry and they remained hidden in the same place. It disembarked and they still stayed crammed in their corners. Ahad's body ached so much that he went into a semi-conscious state.

Seven hours passed, but Ahad did not know. He became aware of a special silence outside. Suddenly the back of the lorry opened. He was dazzled by a shining white landscape. Snow. Teenagers were throwing snowballs at each other, running and laughing. He jumped out, staggered forward, fell down in the snow, stood up again, filled his hands and arms with the soft substance, embraced it, kneaded it and pressed it into balls which he threw in all directions, catching some and soon joining the extraordinary dance.

He danced and danced, and in the bright daylight, he had a dream. In the dream he heard ineffable sounds echoing from mountains and valleys and from every corner of the world. Eagles were flying from every corner of the sky. From everywhere his children and grandchildren came running, and in the convulsions of the earth they sang. Around them the shrieks and screams of fighting and killing kept firing at intervals.

A man was giving a speech, standing in the midst of a group of past and future leaders. They were standing while everything around them was moving. Ahad knew the man's name was Khaled, the Eternal. His voice resonated in the most vibrant tone:

"BROTHERS AND SISTERS WE ARE ONE."

Noha Nasser

I run a social enterprise called MELA with a mission to bridge cultures. In 2015, I wrote a book called Bridging Cultures capturing the intersection between my personal and professional life as a second generation immigrant in the UK and an urban designer. I participated in the creation of this book using my experience volunteering with Refugee Resilience Collective – a group of psychotherapists who travelled weekly to Jules Ferry in Calais to support women and families dealing with the trauma and stress of being a refugee. I supported the team by translating and interpreting Arabic to English.

My experience in the camp was quite profound as I came across such resilient women as well as very determined and well-educated women. I was passionate to tell their stories in a light that reflected that strength and courage – contrary to common media narratives. I also co-founded the Writers Empowerment Club in 2016 – a group of over 25 writers keen to support each other in their publishing endeavours. When the idea for some of the group to explore creative writing came up, I decided it was time to try my hand at a form of writing I hadn't practiced since high school.

Amina, my main character, represents a strong Muslim Sudanese young woman who embarks on a perilous journey to save her family and along the way discovers her sense of self. Her identity is constantly challenged and undermined as parts of her are labelled and rejected; her gender, her race, and her faith. However, Amina stays faithful to who she knows herself to be –an honourable human being. This knowledge is what keeps her hopes alive as she travels across the Sudanese and Libyan desert to Egypt and then to Greece before reaching the Calais' Jungle.

Amina's Diary: a Journey Crossing the Borders to Human Unity

(Photo credited to MHRS Art Vision on unsplash.com)

Date	Event
26 Feb 2003	Conflict in Darfur region of Sudan starts. Kallek is the scene of an atrocious genocide with women being raped and men being tortured and killed by militia.
First quarter of 2013	Renewed inter-tribal conflict.
Early March 2013	Village of Torobeda torched to the ground by Janjaweed militia (Arab Sudanese government-backed militia).
Jan 2015	Calais Jungle comes into being.
Summer 2015	Balkan Route opened as Humanitarian Corridor. Refugees given a registration card called 'khartias' – Greek papers received on arrival.
20 Aug 2015	1st border restriction with Macedonia – laying out of barbed wire fence with military back up.
14 Nov 2015	Fire in The Jungle – fight between Afghans and Sudanese. Sudanese quarter in the Jungle burnt down.
18 Nov 2015	Macedonian border closed again: Syrian, Iraqi and Afghans (SIA) only.
Dec 2015	Idomeni camp evictions with non-SIA sent to Athens.
1 Feb 2016	Church and Mosque demolished in the Jungle to create a security zone.
18 Feb 2016	Afghans restricted from crossing Macedonia.
07 Mar 2016	Council of Europe and Turkey make a 3 billion Euro bilateral agreement recognising Turkey as the first country of asylum. Anyone arriving in Greece is deported to Turkey or unable to leave 'hot spots' (reception centres on the Aegean islands).
08 March 2016	Gates closed permanently on Macedonian border.
12 Mar 2016	March of Hope – 4000 refugees march 6km around the Macedonian border and attempt to cross over a fast flowing river. All captured by armed military officers and forcibly returned to Greece through a hole cut in the fence.
26 May 2016	Inhabitants of Idomeni camp evicted by 1500 riot police and relocated to military camps.
Early October 2016	Rumours of demolition of the Jungle.
25 October 2016	Demolition of The Jungle in Calais.

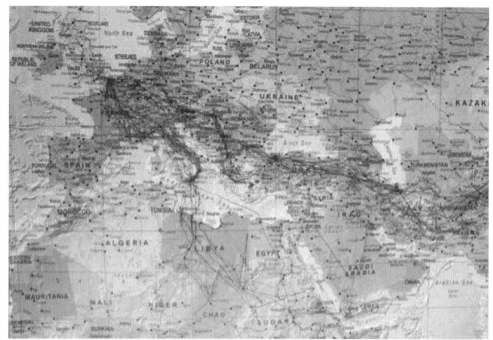

The routes mapped by refugees in the Calais Jungle 2016 produced by the charity 'Art Refuge' (Photo credit: Noha Nasser)

21 February 2003   Torobeda, Sudan

Today is my 11th birthday. Mama has shown me how to wear the hijab because she says I am now a woman. I don't feel like a woman. The hijab isn't very comfortable. It's itchy, especially when I get all sweaty chasing my brothers Mahmood and Ahmed around the fields near the house.

I noticed Mama's friends are all congratulating Mama about my hijab. It must be important to them. Baba looked pleased too, like he was proud of me. Inas wore her hijab last week. She said to me that her Mama had said it now means she can please Allah even more. I really want to please Allah. In my Islamic Studies class, the sheikh said that pleasing Allah is the most important thing any Muslim can do and we can show how much we love Allah by praying, fasting, doing charitable deeds, loving our neighbours and being good people. I know the hijab is one way a girl can be good by protecting her outer beauty and focusing on her inner beauty. It is what all the girls do in Torobeda. The sheikh also said that even though Allah has brought the drought to Darfur we must never stop praying and giving thanks for what we have.

The drought has been difficult on Baba. It's difficult to be thankful for that. His livestock have died of thirst. His plants haven't grown. Baba doesn't look very happy. I have never seen him so anxious. He is anxious about the drought but I think he is also angry at President Bashir. I heard him speaking about the President to his friends when they came over the other evening. They were talking about how the President has turned his back on us because we are an African tribe and not Arabs. I heard Baba talking about how some of our people have joined armies that want to fight against the President's Arab armies. I don't like the sound of fighting. Why can't we talk about it and figure it all out like Baba makes me do when I argue with Mahmood? Baba always said that it is a longstanding tradition for tribes to discuss their problems.

27 February, 2003   Torobeda, Sudan

Something terrible happened in Kallek yesterday. The whole village is talking about it. The villagers all look terrified. Baba came back from a meeting with the elders tonight looking so sad. His eyes were large, bloodshot, and he looked close to tears. His voice was shaking as he spoke to Mama.

He was whispering and had his back to me, but I could just make out he was saying Ammo Bakr and his children were all tortured and killed by the Janjaweed.

I remember Zainab, Ammo Bakr's daughter. She is a year younger than me. Baba took us to visit them for the first time last summer. Me, Mahmood and Ahmed played in the courtyard of their house in Kallek. I remember we found much joy chasing the chickens. I also heard Baba say that Ammo Bakr's wife, Amma Manal, was raped.

What is rape? And who are the Janjaweed Baba is talking about who do all this? It is something dreadful just by the way Baba is speaking. I think there is something sinful about these people and what they do. Mama looks very afraid. She is very impatient with me this evening. I m going to bed early and will pray for Zainab and her family.

21 February 2013   Torobeda, Sudan

Today has been a strange and unexpected 21st birthday. I woke up this morning so excited. I have finally become an adult in the eyes of the Zaghawa tribe. It is a longstanding tradition to celebrate the coming of age. I have been away for two weeks preparing for my new role in society. Today they celebrate me and I get re-integrated into society. I still have to respect my family's traditions and live under Baba's rules, but now I mean something. I am someone with a contribution to make. I am fortunate to study journalism. It is my biggest dream to become the best journalist in Darfur.

We need journalists now, more than ever. I can't keep quiet anymore about the inter-tribal conflict that has erupted in the past few months. The outright discrimination against African Sudanese by Bashir's Arab Sudanese government is a scourge on our deeply-held traditions of resolving conflict peacefully. I have never forgotten the genocide in Kallek. I must find a way to get the international community to hold Bashir and his Janjaweed militia to account for their atrocities. I want to speak up as an African, as a Muslim, and as a woman. I will not be silenced by their torture or by the dishonour they have brought upon our women.

It's now the eighth day the university has been closed. Bashir is afraid of our protests against his injustice. I may not graduate this year because of this disruption. Let him be afraid. I may not have my certificate but I am determined to join the Journalists Without Borders movement. I will continue to report on what's going on. I will not let anything stop me, not even the government's threats of arresting me.

I made the most of not going to the university today. I spent the day with Mama. She gave me one of her big, warm hugs in the morning. She looked into my eyes with concern. She said: "Amina, you are a grown woman now. I worry so much. All your thinking is focused on your political activism. It is too dangerous. Take my advice, my precious daughter. It is time to focus on getting married and having your own family. I have been speaking with Kawsar. Her son Majeed is a good young man. He wants to propose to you this evening."

How was I supposed to react to that? It is customary to marry girls off early. Turning 21, I am considered older than usual. I am not ready. I have my dream to think about. It is impossible to argue with Mama.

This evening after dinner, Majeed arrived with his mother and father. Mama and Baba were all dressed up in their best clothes. Mahmood and Ahmed jeered and laughed at me, calling me 'the bashful bride'. They know that infuriates me. I am not bashful. If anything I am the opposite. Baba always says I am too political and I should think about what I say and when I say it.

It was the most awkward experience. I sat in a new dress Mama had bought me this afternoon, being scrutinised like some kind of commodity. I hate it. Majeed isn't a bad person. But what could he possibly understand about my ambition to become the best journalist in Darfur? What he expects of me is to get my degree and stay at home rearing his children while he goes out to farm the land. Well, that's not going to happen. I won't give up my dreams for anyone – even my family. I will speak to Mama tomorrow and tell her what I think.

22 February 2013   Somewhere in the Darfur wilderness

Oh what a black day. My heart is broken. Mahmood woke me this morning with his loud shouting. The house was a chaotic frenzy of movement. I was confused. I demanded an explanation. No one answered me. We gathered our basic clothing into rucksacks.

We ran out of the house into the corn fields behind. Mahmood was leading. He was impatiently herding us along, forcing us to duck our heads below the tall, confident stalks of the familiar golden corn tassels. I had grown up all my life with the cornfields around our house. They had fed us. But I had never before thought about how this wonderful plant could offer so much shelter and protection. I am grateful we were able to escape. My heart has not stopped racing since the morning. I can't settle down to sleep on this rocky ground near the river. I have never slept in the open before.

As I lie here, I close my tear-filled eyes tonight holding the last scenes of my beloved Torobeda. The beautiful village where I grew up. My people are all gone, obliterated. In my mind's eye, I breathe again the choking, thick, dark smoke that hung heavily in the air as we escaped. I see the vision of the fire engulfing the whole village. I catch sight of Amma Basmaand her young daughters being dragged violently by their hair into the bushes by the Janjaweed. I can't bear to look. Allah save us.

4 March 2013   Saraf Omra Refugee Camp, Sudanese border with Chad

Today we finally reach Saraf Omra Refugee Camp on the border with Chad. It is my new home. I have not stopped walking for weeks. My feet are chaffed and blistered from the rubbing of my sandals against the trapped sand grains. My clothes are bedraggled, enveloped by a thick film of sweat and dirt. I have not showered. It is a relief to stop and rest now.

My new home is nothing more than sand-swept monotonous lines of endless, flapping, blue and white tents. Families are sitting outside around their cooking fires to escape the heat trapped under the plastic covers. Kids with unwashed faces and hands are playing hide and seek between the tents, laughing in spite of the uncertain fate of their parents. I see sullen women carrying big jars of water on their heads. Men leave early to go in search of firewood. People have vacant looks in their eyes.

With nowhere else to be safe in Darfur, there is little choice but to stay in Saraf Omra. The refugee camp is run by the United Nations High Commissioner for Refugees. The UNHCR's humanitarian assistance is something I have known about. Even though I am grateful for their help, I am also deeply frustrated. Is aid the only contribution the international community can make? Do we not deserve more? What about our human rights? Our right to life? Our right to freedom from torture? Our right to equality? What about the international community's political influence? Why aren't they doing anything about Bashir?

Bashir calls himself a Muslim. He's not a Muslim. He is a tyrant. What he did in Kallek never leaves me. The sheikh taught me we are a Muslim Umma, one shared Muslim humanity. It is lies. How can Muslim kill Muslim under the evil guise of race?

This is my land and the land of my ancestors. I am African. I am proud to be from the Zaghawa tribe. We toiled the lands of Darfur before Islam, even before Sudan was created. Bashir thinks he can simply reject what connects me with this land, my African-ness. His cruel actions crush what ties me to him; my Muslim-ness and my Sudanese-ness. I am all these elements in one. Bashir cannot separate me into bits, accepting parts of me and rejecting others. I will not let him.

The sheikh told me we are one humanity. I am part of this ONE humanity. It cannot be fiction if it is in the holy Quran. Baba says the Quran holds the truth. I remember a verse of the Quran Baba always recited:

O Humanity! Without doubt We have created you from a male and a female and have made you into various nations and tribes, so that you may come to know and understand one another. Definitely the most honoured among you in the sight of Allah is the one who is the most Allah-Conscious. Surely Allah has full Knowledge and is All-Aware.

I look around me. I see a desolate place teeming with humanity. Where are those conscious of Allah? Where are the honourable ones? We are one humanity. We deserve more than to survive. We deserve the opportunity to fulfil our greatest individual and collective potential. I am making a pledge today. I dedicate my life to the mission of freeing humanity from the illusion of our fragmentation.

21 March 2013   Saraf Omra Refugee Camp, Sudan

Life in Saraf Omra is taking its toll. Mama and Baba's health has deteriorated. They both look haggard. Baba is quiet and withdrawn. He misses Torobeda and his life tilling the fields. I remember images of his face; his sweet, wise smile when he would come back from a day farming the fields. That twinkle in his eye. I knew it was a measure of his affection for me. Today, that twinkle is extinguished. He spends his days in quiet contemplation, hardly eating anything.

Mama, the woman I always looked up to. Her feistiness and determination is replaced with depression. She is a woman who believes deeply in justice. The cruelty and humiliation she witnessed has broken her faith. She spends her day walking to the water distribution point to get jars of water or gathering wood for the fire when Baba is too weak.

My family is wasting away here. I am making myself helpful around the camp. I am helping with the repatriation of Sudanese families coming from Chad. We provide them with tents and food. Today, I met Majeed at the UNHCR office. His big smile unwrinkled his weather-beaten face. He is volunteering too. He has lost a lot of weight. His mother died in the razing of Torobeda. His father was captured by the militia. I had an urge to embrace him, but stopped myself. I took his two hands in mine and held his gaze. All I could offer him was our silence.

I see many young people like me, Mahmood, Ahmed and Majeed around the camp. What does the future hold for these bright young men and women? Will I ever become the best journalist in Darfur? Is this going to be my life? I pray to Allah to guide me.

22 March 2013   Saraf Omra Refugee Camp, Sudan

Allah has answered my prayers. I met Abdo. He seems trustworthy. He has helped several people leave the camp and find safe passage to Libya. They cross on boats to Europe. Europe means freedom and safety.

From the UK, I could help Mama, Baba, Mahmood and Ahmed. I could help them find a good, safe life. Ammo Omer, mother's brother, lives in the UK. He will look after us.

How to pay Abdo the $1000 to escape the camp? It's a lot of money. Some women are working hard labour on surrounding farms. The dangers many of these women are facing are known. They are raped and dishonoured. Do I have any choice? I will risk it. The sooner I leave the better. Allah give me strength.

26 March, 2013   Saraf Omra Refugee Camp, Sudan

I have broken the news to Baba, Mama and Mahmood. I told them I want to work in the farms. They were up in arms!

I had to tell them the truth about Europe. Baba started shouting at me. He swore to Allah it would be over his dead body. Mama called me 'wild and crazy'.

Only Mahmood understands my plan. This is the only way to change our fate. He is proud of my courage, but he won't leave me. He is coming with me.

Over dinner, Mahmood and I told Mama and Baba about our decision. They cried. But they see the determination in our hearts. We embraced, then sat together holding hands around the fire. We sat for a while in deep silence, the flames dancing with the wind. The same fire ignited in my heart for the winds heading to Europe. My family's salvation. Escape is our only solution. Mama and Baba blessed us. Mama gave us all her gold bracelets to sell for the $2000 we need to get to Libya and to cross the sea.

I am in conflict. I will leave the relative safety and routine of the camp. At the same time, I am going to have to do something different to change our lives. I shake with uncertainty. All I know, is there is no turning back. May Allah guide me and Mahmood.

14 April 2013   Libyan Desert

I cannot stop my tears. I have failed. I have been captured. I am in a dark, smelly cell with two other women and their babies. Where is Mahmood? Where is he? Will I ever see him again?

I am a fool thinking I could save my family.

I am angry at Abdo. He deserted us. He handed us over to two men in pickup trucks in the middle of the Libyan desert this morning at dawn. We did not eat or drink anything for days. We walked under the eerie cover of darkness to avoid discovery. Abdo betrayed me. Why did I trust him? He promised to take us to Tripoli and another agent, Amar, would put me and Mahmood on boats to cross to Italy.

They took Mahmood from me. They prised his hands out of mine. I shouldn't have let him go. I should have hung on like my life depended on it. Could I have done more? Said something? I know it was impossible. The two henchmen were far stronger than me. I can hear Mahmood howling; "Leave my sister alone!" Hisface was distraught and contorted. I closed my eyes and prayed Allah reunites us. Pleas e Allah, let me set eyes on Mahmood again.

18 April 2013   a detention camp near Tripoli, Libya

The stone floor was cold and hard beneath me. I felt paralysed. I can still smell his acrid sweat on my clothes. Tears are falling uncontrollably from the corners of my eyes, soaking my veil. I weep for the loss of my honour. The tide of senseless violence against women. Is it just another price to pay for my freedom and my family's?

I am a woman. An honourable woman destined to be the best journalist in Darfur. You want to shatter me. To rob me of my destiny? I may be physically weaker, but I am a volcano of inner strength. You have taken what is mine through brute force, but you have not taken my soul. That is mine no matter what.

I will find the strength to nurse my broken and bruised body. Time will find a way to heal me outside and in. Time to forgive and forget the tyranny of man.

I do not understand how a Muslim man can violate a Muslim woman in this barbaric manner. I know that this is not how Allah guides us. I recite the Holy Quran to myself:

Lodge [women] where you dwell out of your means and do not harm them in order to oppress them.

These are not Muslim men. They are animals, controlled by their carnal desire to dominate their prey. Their superficial acts of strength, camouflage an emptiness inside them. I pray Allah forgives my perpetrator and forgives me.

6 June 2015   Cairo, Egypt

It's been a year since entering Egypt on that rickety bus along the desert road from Tripoli to Cairo. Today my heart has been stirred. My flatmate, Raheema, says there is a new way to get to northern Europe through the Balkan route. It has recently opened. It means I will have to find passage across the Mediterranean to Greece, then make my way up to Macedonia, and across Europe. Raheema says there are many already making this journey.

My thoughts wander to Mahmood. Did he manage to escape the Libyan gangs? Did he cross the Mediterranean and get to Italy? No one knows where he is. I send a short, loving prayer to him.

I recollect my escape from the Libyan mafia prison on that moonless night. I had to hide in the bush from the roving torchlights of my perpetrators. I am grateful to the Libyan family who took me in and put me on a bus to Egypt. Cairo is a good home. This big, dusty city is alive with the throngs of millions of people finding a way to make a living. This ancient city subsumes humanity within its embrace.

I love my work for Madam Fawzia. She is kind. The wage is not good, but I am grateful I can save. Thanks to Raheema who has taken me under her wing. Our rooftop shack isn't much. From here we overlook the distinctive Cairo skyline at sunrise. I can just make out the Pyramids in the distance. Between the buildings I watch how the Nile works her magic as she cuts through the dense jungle of concrete that lines her banks. She shimmers, brightening the already clear sky. The noise of car horns signals the dragon awakening from the cover of night.

I will not rest until I get to Ammo Omer in Leicester. Raheema and her children are like my family now. It will be hard to leave them. At least in Egypt, refugees have freedom of movement and don't have to live in camps. I admire Raheema's patience for her application for asylum to be processed by the UNHCR. Her husband waits in Sudan.

I have no desire to seek asylum here. My passion to find Mahmood and to go to Ammo Omer still burns brightly in my heart. Cairo has healed mefrom what happened in Libya. The opening of the Balkan route is a sign. Allah is telling me to finish what I started.

17 January 2016   Crossing the Mediterranean

The sky was pitch dark and the spray from the waves kept hitting my face. I gasped for air. I spent the night on the migrant rescue patrol ship, Aquarius. I shivered with cold and shock. The blankets had not made a difference. Rescue staff gave me hot soup to calm me down. The bright lights focused on the engulfing darkness of the surrounding high sea as we rocked up and down violently. Limp bodies were being hoisted on board, many of them I recognised; babies, children, young women and men. I felt like being sick.

The swells of the waves grew and grew after leaving Rosetta. Ringing in my ears were the screams of the mothers holding their babies tight. Men raised their voices in chorus reciting 'Allah Akbar'.

The boat had made a loud hollow ringing sound as a wave hit our side. Thoughts gripped me of Mama, Baba, Mahmood and Ahmed. Would I ever see them again? I started to sob.

I crashed into the water. It was dark and cold. The overbearing waves hit against me like I was a piece of balsa wood. The waves covered my head as I gasped for air. The cries for help of people around me drowned out momentarily as I disappeared into the sea's mighty grasp.

I must have lost consciousness. I was sinking further away from the surface of the tumultuous water. Down, down, down I had sunk into the depths of the darkness with no breath left.

Elias, the rescue worker, said he spotted my white head scarf and fished me out. Thanks to Allah. Allah Akbar! I have been given new life. So many lives have been taken. I give gratitude as I remember the words of the Holy Quran:

How can you disbelieve in Allah when you were lifeless and He brought you to life; then He will cause you to die, then He will bring you back to life, and then to Him you will be returned.

With this new life, I promise to do good and absolve those souls that were returned to Allah today. I pray for their souls as I arrive in Athens Port.

2 March 2016   Idomeni Refugee Camp, Macedonia Border

She was no more than 12 years of age. We were queuing at the soup kitchen. The mud was thicker today. It hadn't stopped raining all night. There must have been a large influx of arrivals last night - the queue was almost twice as long. I prayed there would be enough food for all of us. I took my place in the queue and a wave of acceptance came over me as I patiently waited in line. The rain started to get heavier. This will test my patience, I knew.

My thoughts were pierced by the aid worker shouting out "Nothing left, it is all gone!" I couldn't believe it, I was only four people away from the window. My heart sank again. The girl in front of me started to sob. I reached out to put my arm around her shoulder. Without hesitation she buried her wet face into my chest. We stayed in this strange, yet comfortable, embrace for what seemed like a long time. I felt an immediate bond with this scrawny, teary-eyed young girl. What was it about her? Was it her innocence? Her youth? Her vulnerability? Something in her reached out to me.

I slowly guided her away. I looked ahead and there was some commotion by the gates. The young girl asked a passer-by "What's going on?" I noticed she had a Syrian English accent. Her voice was meek. "It's the bread man," came the response, "he brings us bread that he cannot sell". I gave a sigh of relief. This is a small miracle. We walked up to this short, rotund elderly man. His eyes were full of kindness and his smile warm and loving. He looked at us "Here you are, this is the last large loaf I have." The young girl clutched his hand and started kissing it. "Thank you, thank you" she cried. "Just a minute", the baker looked into his van and came out carrying a jam cake. "Here you are. I come every day at about this time. I give away what is not sold in my shop. Tomorrow is Saturday, so if you want bread tomorrow, make sure you are here, as I do not come on Sundays." The young girl covered the bread and cake with a waterproof. She turned to me with her forlorn eyes. "Thank you so much for being so kind, and I don't even know your name?" She told me her name is Rubina. I smiled at her warmly, "I am Amina." She unwrapped the loaf of bread and broke a piece off for me. I embraced her more strongly. She took my hand in a playful way, and in the rain, she pulled me across the muddy ground to where her tent was pitched.

Idomeni Camp on the Macedonian border had built up a reputation for being the last bastion of Europe stemming the tide of refugees fleeing war-torn countries. Conditions were very bad. The rain and the mud didn't help. People camped in flimsy water-logged tents by the railway, hoping they could find refuge in the slow moving trains heading over the borders. The Greeks were more lenient than the Macedonians, I had heard. The Greek 'khartia' ID card I got in Athens allowed me to travel in the country up to the Macedonian border. My primary task was to find an agent to get me across. Other refugees said that Macedonians kept closing the border. In November they closed the border and allowed only Syrians, Iraqis and Afghanis through. They called them SIAs. Then they evicted non-SIAs a month later and sent them back to Athens. I am the only dark face here. Not many Sudanese come this route. There are also very few women travelling alone. I met one or two Afghani women. They kept themselves to themselves.

Rubina is the only person who has really connected with me.

3 March 2016   Idomeni Refugee Camp, Macedonian Border

I have gotten to know Rubina better. I entered her tent and saw a small boy and girl huddled together sleeping in the corner of their cramped temporary home. "My brother and sister" she whispered. I smiled and tears welled up in my eyes as I remembered Ahmed and Mahmood. I prayed they were both safe. We took our shoes off and sat down on her bed to share out the cake. I put down the piece of cardboard I had collected and sat down beside her. She looked at me inquisitively. I noticed her dainty features; long mousy full-bodied brown hair, large green eyes, fair skin, a small nose, and thin lips. She was beautiful.

"I come from Syria," she said. "And you?"
"I am from Sudan."

52

"Ah Sudan. I haven't seen many Sudanese people here. We have come through Turkey. It has been a very difficult journey,"Rubina stated.

"I came through Egypt. Yes, everyone's journey has been difficult," I sighed.

Rubina started to cry again:

"My mother died after leaving Syria. My father took it so badly. He is very depressed. We left all our life behind in Syria."

"I am so sorry to hear that. Is it just you, your father and your brother and sister travelling?" I asked.

"Yes. My father started drinking. I don't know how to help him." She started to cry harder now. I put my arm around her. "It's ok," I reassured her. "Everything will work out in the end, have faith." That's what my mother used to say and here I was saying it back.

Maybe what connected me with this young girl was she reminded me of me. I looked at her. She was young to have taken on so much hardship and responsibility. I was 11 when the war in Darfur had erupted. I too had felt compelled to grow up sooner than I had wanted. My father was a successful farmer and herder who had status amongst our tribal clan. My mother also had her position as a tribal organiser with the other women in the village. Life was stable. It all changed overnight.

Rubina touched my hand and brought me back to the moment. She started to smile. "It's nice to be able to speak to someone about what happened. I haven't spoken to anyone since my mother died."
I smiled back. "Well you are not alone. As long as I am here, you have a friend." We held hands.

The tent flap opened, and a man crawled into the tent. He seemed tense. It was Rubina's father. He seemed distraught because he couldn't get hold of alcohol. He asked Rubina to help him. He started to sob when he mentioned his deceased wife. My heart sank for the cruelty of war. Allah help this father to look after his children.

7 March 2016   Idomeni Refugee Camp, Macedonian Border

I was woken by a commotion outside. I hardly slept with the persistent sound of raindrops hitting the plastic top. I was cold and shivery. My thoughts went to Rubina and her family. Since meeting her father a few days ago I could tell she was the one holding the family together. Her father seemed lost in his own thoughts, probably under the influence of alcohol. It must be difficult to have been a doctor in Syria one minute then to find himself living in such squalor the next. And losing his wife. Life can be cruel and dramatic. Then I remembered an important verse of the Quran:

And we removed from you your burden which had weighed upon your back.

And raised high for you your repute. For indeed with hardship will be ease.

Indeed, with hardship will be ease.

For Allah knows best and knows that we may think life is cruel but at the same time Allah saves us from a worse fate. I must be grateful. I don't know what Allah knows. I must trust that when Allah closes a door, Allah opens a window.

I was alerted by the shouting growing louder as more people emerged from their tents. "Europe has closed its borders today. You can't travel to Macedonia," shouted a young man from the UNHCR.

A crowd of people had gathered around him. Tensions were high. The young man looked afraid of the mob. He was only the messenger. We joined the crowd. Some men shouted abuse at the European Union. "Cowards, cowards! How can they forget about us and our plight?" They shouted. Women carrying children started to cry "What will happen to us?" I found Rubina in the crowd and held her hand tight.

This news was shattering. I had waited years to get to this point. I couldn't be turned away now. What had happened? I heard people talking about Turkey's bilateral agreement with the Council of Europe for 3 billion euros the day before. Turkey had agreed to be recognised as the first country of asylum for refugees. According to the Dublin Agreement, at the first port of arrival, refugees had to declare asylum. What had been happening during the crisis was that thousands of refugees had not. They were set on reaching destinations further north like

Sweden, Germany and the UK. I was one of them. Even though I picked up my khartias in Athens, I had not declared asylum. The agreement with Turkey meant

those refugees arriving in Greece would be deported back to Turkey, or were to be held at the reception centres in the hotspots on the Aegean Islands. I needed to find a solution.

I went to sit down. Rubina sat down next to me. Her face looked confused and anxious. "I don't understand." She said. I tried to explain and she put her head in her hands, shaking it from side to side.

In the camp, men were getting very angry. There was shouting and swearing. "We are stuck! What are we supposed to do, just stay here and die? What about our children? Do they not have a heart?" The volunteers and aid workers did their best to calm people down. "Another way will open up. Stay calm."

Rumours began to spread around the camp of a protest march. A number of Syrian men had called people to action. "We will force ourselves across the border!" they proclaimed. "If we can't go through the border, we will go around the border!" I got to know a few of the Arabic-speaking Iraqi and Syrian women who were travelling with their husbands. They told me it would be a difficult walk, about 6 kilometres around the border. They would also have to cross a fast flowing river. People seemed determined, many of them unable to accept the idea of remaining in Greece in the military camps. I too felt an urge to move forward. I had been through too much to stop now. Allah give me courage and keep me safe.

12 March 2016   March of Hope, Macedonia Border

They called it the March of Hope. We got up early today. About 4000 people had gathered in the camp carrying their tents, their bags, and children on their backs. It was rainy. The mud seemed especially bad because of the number of people walking across the fields. I met up with Rubina's family near the Hara Hotel. Rubina's father seemed disillusioned. His eyes seemed absent. I had seen that look before in Saraf Omra. It was a look of despair, overwhelm, fear and stress rolled into one. I could see Rubina holding her brother and sister's hands tightly and holding them close. She spoke to them encouragingly. They followed their father a few steps behind as he followed the crowds.

By midday the rain had subsided and people sat down for lunch. Journalists were everywhere taking photographs of us, as if we were objects of amusement. Go away. My dreams of being the best journalist in Darfur flooded back. This type of journalism is unethical. They are recording our indignity. Why aren't these journalists changing the minds of the European people? Am I placing too much responsibility on the shoulders of journalists? It is the politicians that are accountable for Fortress Europe.

Europe's hostile response to our plight was getting worse by the day. They are afraid of Muslims living amongst them. It is a historical thing. Being a Muslim in the 21st century is some kind of curse. Even within the Muslim Umma, there is violence between Muslims. The genocide in Darfur and the violence against me in Libya gripped me. A deep sickening feeling in the pit of my stomach rose. Even on the shores of liberal Europe – my Muslim-ness has been called into question. My headscarf attracts ridicule and suspicion. One elderly Greek man in a small village on my way up from Athens to Macedonia pushed me off the bus, telling me to 'go away'. Is there nowhere where I can just be who I am? Myself? I recall a verse of the Quran:

Say: O disbelievers!

I worship not that which ye worship;

Nor worship ye that which I worship.

And I shall not worship that which ye worship.

Nor will ye worship that which I worship.

Unto you your religion, and unto me my religion.

In the Quran, it says anyone can practise their own faith freely. I embrace my many facets and my many qualities. I am unique. I have a contribution to make regardless of what I believe and how I dress. In this Christian territory, I am feared. The European rejection of me runs deep in the European psyche. They have built kilometres of barbed wire fences to keep me out.

Today I marched for hope. Hope that one day I can prove to the Europeans I am just like them. I dream to be a journalist. I believe in social justice. I want to save my family from a dead-end fate. I want to build my own life. Become something.

Do good. I want to make a difference. I am not to be feared. I am to be embraced and welcomed. Allah, "open their eyes and hearts."

13 March 2016   Idomeni Refugee Camp, Macedonian Border

I don't know where Rubina is. I am worried for her and her family. I am back in Idomeni after failing to get across the river.

The hole in the barbed-wire fence had allowed us to trickle through. Our clothes got caught on the barbed wire. That didn't slow us down. As we approached the river, people slowed down. It looked treacherous. The rains had sent large volumes of water down off the mountains. The water looked like it was churning. It was a muddy brown colour. People started to cross tentatively. The braver of us raised their arms above their heads carrying their heavy bags. Sometimes they lost their balance and would slip into the water, losing their bags as they floated down the river. I closed my eyes in dread. Images of my Mediterranean crossing paralysed me.

I looked at Rubina and told her I couldn't do it. She reached out and held my hand, her sullen eyes staring at me. "Listen to me Amina. You can cross this river. We will cross together. Everything will work out in the end, have faith." I opened my eyes. She was quoting my mother's wise words. I pictured my mother's face. I knew she was anxiously waiting for news from me. I was unable to call them for over two weeks. They must be worried, I thought. 'I can do this,' I whispered to myself. "I have to do this, for my family." I repeated. I removed my rucksack and slowly raised it over my head as I cautiously stepped into the cold current of the river.

People had created a line. They slowly fought the torrents, doing their best not to lose their balance. One small step at a time. At one point, the water reached my chin. I looked up at the angry grey sky. For a moment, I was looking down at myself. Just a face poking above the muddy, brown, churning water. I neared the other side. Out of the woods appeared armed military officers. They were on horses. They rounded those of us who had crossed. They had batons and were beating people. I tried to run towards the woods, calling to Rubina to follow me. But as we were about to reach the edge of the woods, a large black horse came up beside me. A hand grabbed my headscarf and pulled me back. I fell to the ground. Another officer ran up and began to beat me with his baton. I screamed in pain. Rubina tried to stop him but he pushed her to one side. "Stop!" I yelled. I cowered away to minimise the areas he could hurt me. He eventually stopped, dragging me through the mud and then pushing me into the river.

I found myself floating down, my body in too much pain to stop myself. The river turned a bend. A man reached out his hand from the riverbank and I grabbed it. He pulled me to safety. I sat on the bank, coughing and shivering from the ordeal I had just experienced. The army officers were everywhere, forcing us to return through the hole in the fence back to Idomeni. So now I am back here praying that Rubina has managed to get away. I have decided to find an agent in Athens who can fly me to France. I can't make this journey on my own.

28 June 2016 The Jungle, Calais, France

I have arrived at the infamous Zhangal in Calais. It is known around the world as the corrupted version, 'Jungle'. 'Zhangal' is in fact an Afghani

Pashto word that means forest. I arrived this morning after days of walking from Paris. My flight from Athens to Paris on my fake passport was cleverly organised by Gabriel. I wished I could have flown direct to the UK but he could only get me a Schengen entry port. He was a good agent. It cost me $1500. A good price.

The French CRS police guard the Jungle. They stopped me and asked for my papers. I am ready for their hostility. I have run into them before. They speak maliciously. Why is it so personal with them? What prejudice drives them? I look into their eyes. They must have families too. They must have moments of vulnerability like us all. A wave of compassion flows between me and them. They have been given orders they are obeying. They are conditioned to hate me. It's not their fault. I take a step back and patiently wait until they let me pass. They wave me towards the end of the winding road that leads to the tent city. I check in at the Women and Children's Centre, Jules Ferry. I saw fellow Sudanese men gathering in the woods next to the tent city. They are making phone calls on their mobile phones and hanging out their washing. They are bored. I dare not speak with them. I keep my eyes down.

I entered the makeshift streets that I have heard so much about. Heaps of heels, baby shoes, abandoned teddy bears and soaked duvets line the rubbish-strewn muddy paths. I noticed the same forlorn faces I saw in Saraf Omra. Some live in tents. Others are more resourceful and build temporary structures of lightweight timber and awnings. There is an entire area where people are living in shipping containers. It is surrounded by fencing and has special entry for those who have sought asylum in France and are processing their claims.

Flags from all around the world are flying in every corner of this camp; Sudan, Iran, Pakistan, Kurdistan, Afghanistan, Syria, Egypt, Eritrea, Ethiopia and many more. I notice they aren't all mixed up. The different nationalities group together creating their own quarter. Is it out of fear or choice? Even the shops along the central pedestrian route symbolise the different nations.

Graffiti on the makeshift buildings and on banners describe the range of messages. Some are resistance like 'No Justice' and 'Fight Police'. Some are hopeful: 'Ya Allah'. Some capture people's dreams: 'We just want to go in England PLEASE'.

Two women walk towards me. One is pregnant. They are from Eritrea. They look at me with suspicion. Is this a place where no one trusts anyone? I heard about the violence that erupted between the Sudanese and Afghanis on 27 May. Five charity workers, two police officers and more than 30 migrants had been injured when fighting broke out. A good part of the Sudanese quarter had been razed to the ground. The Sudanese are being persecuted everywhere - at home and abroad. But these people share one goal. Why aren't they collaborating?

The Women and Children's Centre has been set up to guarantee the security of the 400 women, girls and children in Zhangal. The compound was heavily gated with barbed wire. I saw a few women hanging out their washing. I asked them to let me in. They called the supervisor. A European-looking woman opened the gate and asked me if I have just arrived. She ushered me in. This compound is much better than the camp itself. It is clean, and women and children live in well-built temporary buildings. There is a washing room on the corner. Children on bicycles play carefree, chasing each other. The main dining hall has paintings and sketches hung up on the walls, signs that the women and children are getting classes.

I was led into a small office and there sat a gentleman. Behind him were charts with timetables and logistical lists. It looked quite an operation.
He spoke to me politely. I was grateful for that.

After seeing my papers, he showed me to one of the huge tunnel tents that occupied a good part of the grounds. I sighed, no real bed in the porta-cabins for me. I was too exhausted to argue. I just wanted a place to settle my head and put my feet up. They were sore. He pulled away the thick plastic drapes that sealed the tent. It was dark inside and it took me some time for my eyes to adjust. The tent was quite empty. A few sleeping bags were laid out along one side. I made out a figure sitting hunched in the corner. That silhouette looked familiar. I walked up to the figure and kneeled down. How could I forget that long mousy full-bodied brown hair, large green eyes, fair skin, small nose, and thin lips. She was beautiful. My darling Rubina turned her face towards me. For a moment she looked confused. Then like the sun coming out from behind the clouds, her face transformed into a huge smile. We fell into each other's arms. I did not let go. We finally stood up. She pointed to her young brother and sister sleeping. I couldn't wait to spend time with them again.

I am grateful to Allah for returning my Rubina to me.

4 July 2016   The Jungle, Calais, France

It has been my luckiest day for a very long time. I met Rubina's father at the Afghani restaurant in the main High Street of the Jungle. I heard it was an important meeting place where the elders of the different communities discussed how they can co-exist here. A tradition we have always upheld back in Darfur. I smiled.

The High Street is full of shops. All sizes. They sell everything. It is like a vibrant market place. I find people resourceful. They make a life with very little. The Jungle was formed in January 2015. Thousands of people have come through this place. Many have stayed refusing to declare asylum in France. People don't want to seek asylum in France because of their track record in rejecting asylum claims. Refugees choose to endure the harsh conditions of this shanty town. Most people want to cross to the UK, like me.

Rubina's father took me into his arms when he saw me. I had missed him. He was more alert than when I had last seen him in Idomeni. The Idomeni camp closed

down a few weeks after I had left. Everyone had been evicted in May. That place had embodied the hope of many people wanting to make a life in Europe. Now it was all gone. But has their hope? I look around me and see that it hasn't.

In the Afghani restaurant, we sit down for a meal of beans and rice. Rubina's father told me about the number of times they had waited for 'Dugar', the traffic jams of lorries waiting to cross The English Channel. 'Dugar' was the time when they can jump on to the lorry. He wanted me to cross with them. He offered to pay for me. I was grateful for his generosity.

I noticed him across the restaurant. A young man serving customers. He was very slim. There was no way I would not notice those endearing features, the soft eyes and full lips that I grew up with in Torobeda, the little boy I had chased around the corn fields at the back of the house. The young man who had had the courage to follow my plan to make our way to Ammo Omer in the UK. I yelped with joy.

The young man looked startled. He turned to me and stood there paralysed. His jaw dropped and his eyes grew wide in disbelief. Tears began to fall down his cheeks. I lost control of all time and space. I pushed back my stool and found myself in his arms. "My dearest Mahmood." Thank you Allah for keeping my faith. Thank you Allah for returning Mahmood to me.

6 October 2016   Crossing the English Channel

It was pitch dark. The smell of onions filled my lungs and nostrils. I prayed the smell would divert the attention of the dogs. I hid behind some big cardboard boxes. Rubina's hand was locked in mine. I heard her breathing sharply and nervously. The lorry was slowing. The dogs barked outside. The scratchy noises reverberated around the lorry as they clambered up the sides of the lorry.

I diverted my attention. I thought of Mahmood. He had made the crossing last week. He called me from Ammo Omer's place in Leicester. His voice was cheerful. I closed my eyes and recited a verse of the Quran:

Allah hath set a seal on their hearts and on their hearing, and on their eyes is a veil; great is the penalty they incur.

The lorry door opened. The light caught the spaces between the boxes. I held my breath and squeezed Rubina's hand. I recited the verse in my head over and over again. The minutes felt like hours. I dared not breathe. The lorry doors slammed shut.

Diane Hands

My name is Diane Hands. I have a wonderful husband, and we have three daughters and four grandchildren. Whilst participating in the Team Management and Leadership Programme at Landmark Worldwide in London I met Brigitte, Doug and Noha. During this course I created 'I Have A Voice Too!', a charity for adults who have special needs and learning difficulties. This fills a gap because many of the activities they used to attend now have age limits.

We have drama workshops on Saturday afternoons where we produce plays and films under professional direction and a monthly crafts and afternoon tea activity. Items made are sold on a charity market stall.

On 30th March 2019 I was privileged to open the National Paralympic Heritage Centre with Paralympian John Harris. The 'I Have a Voice Too!' drama group acted a short play entitled "Dr Guttmann's Journey - Germany to Stoke Mandeville". This was performed three times during the day. Dr Guttmann and his family came to England in 1939 as Jewish Refugees. His method of treating patients with Spinal Injuries and missing limbs was revolutionary. Quote from Sir Ludwig Guttmann, *"If I ever did one good thing in my medical career it was to introduce sport into the rehabilitation of disabled people."* His legacy is the Paralympic Games.

In November 2016 I had a stroke while driving my car which left me with a few problems. I have what is called dyspraxia where I put clothes on upside down or inside out which can look quite funny. Another challenge was teaching myself to read again. So I felt very pleased when I was asked to take part in writing a story for the book Human Crossings.

On the day our stories were completed it was announced in my church that a Friendship Centre is to be opened in Wembley, West London, where refugees can go to be helped with settling into the UK. Various groups will be using one of our chapels to facilitate this.

Rubina's Story: Riches to Rags to Riches

(Photo credit: Ilho Lee, unsplash.com)

Getting ready to leave

I am lying on my bed absorbed in my book when there is a knock on the door and my father enters. He says, "Rubina, I am sorry it's time to leave. I realize this is going to be hard for everyone, especially for your mother with the new baby but as I said yesterday I feel it would be foolish to stay.

"My hospital has been destroyed, luckily we have survived but now I have no work, so it is better that we leave. We have been fortunate in many ways to have seen this possibility coming and been able to prepare for it. I promised my father many years ago that if I needed to leave here I would seek refuge in England. Rubina, try to understand why it has to be this way and be a help and support to your mother.

"Go now and get your brother and sister to finish packing what they want to take with them. Please make sure they put some extra essential clothes in their bags. That way we won't have to unpack the trailer until we are well on our way. I'll go now and help your mother."

I cry, "I don't want to leave. Can't I stay with Maya? She will look after me. Then I won't have to leave this house. Please, please. I don't want to go to England. I don't know anyone in England."

Father responds, "We leave as a family. No arguments. Get ready now."

I run from my room, tears streaming down my face and burst into my sister's room shouting, "Get ready to leave NOW. Put extra clothes in your bag."

My sister Rosarita is only 6; she whines, "Please help me Rubina, I don't know what to take."

"OK, I'll go and tell Sayid and come back," I snap. "Start getting what you want to take ready. You can't take everything."

I enter Sayid's room rather more quietly and say to him, "We are leaving NOW. Get ready."

Sayid baulks, "No, I won't."

I say gently, "Do as I say or father will be really angry. Pack some extra clothes too. I'm just going to help Rosarita, I'll be back. I do not want to leave either but Father is adamant we are leaving. He told us yesterday the hospital had been bombed and he wouldn't have any work now."

"But we are safe here," Sayid answers.

"Come on, just do as you are told," Father shouts from the kitchen, "No arguing. We are leaving as a family today."

Some time later when we enter the kitchen we find our parents hugging each other, and they are both crying. Father looks at us and asks, "Are you all ready?"

"Yes, but do we have to leave? Maya could take care of us. She's still going to be living here."

"We have thought about that and I am sorry to say no."

My father gives Maya a large envelope saying, "These are all the documents for this house. It also gives you permission to have other members of your family live here too. I know you will take care of it for us. We will keep in touch and look forward to seeing you again one day. Now it is time for us to go."

Maya hugs each of us before we go out into the garage and get into the truck. Father starts the engine, the garage doors open, and we drive out into the sunshine.

I cannot resist one last look at our home and thinking 'Will I ever see it again?' Maya is standing on the front steps, waving as we leave. I can't help feeling I want to cry as I sit between Sayid and Rosarita. Something about the way she snuggles up clutching the fur dog that goes everywhere with her irritates me.

At the end of the street the devastation starts. Houses and shops are piles of rubble with some people searching the damage, maybe for their families, maybe to see what can be salvaged. As we past the hospital where Father used to work he started to talk;

"We will not be poor when we arrive in England. I have put money into my English bank account for years. There's enough for a small house and living expenses until I get a job.

"We're just so very lucky, we have money, not just in England. We have money and property here too but when we will be able to use it is an unanswerable question. I inherited many possessions and property from my father, a lot of them I turned into cash and put it in my English bank account. We must never forget to be thankful for all the blessings we receive."

Father continues, "My friend Ken is looking into what is available for me as a job; doctors are always needed. It will be different from here, but we can make it our home. Until we buy a property or decide where we will live Ken will find us some temporary accommodation but our first few nights in England will be spent with Ken and his family.

The first day on the road

Our journey to Greece has begun. Usually when we travel I'm interested in the landscape we're passing through and eagerly looking forward to our destination. Not today. Pulling my coat around me I am determined to block out everything by sleeping. Sleep is a long time in coming.

Some time later I wake up and ask, "Where are we? Who's crying?"

Mother replies, "Your little brother is hungry, and he just wants to make sure we know it. Could we stop for a while, Nizar? I can feed Sami, and I am sure the others could do with stretching their legs."

Father says, "If that's what you want to do. I am feeling a little tired." He drives the truck off the road and says, "Don't go wandering off, children. Make sure you can see us from wherever you are."

The three of us wander about silently, immersed in our own thoughts. We want to be back in our home but I know that's not going to happen. Why can't I accept that?

Hearing Father call us we go back to our parents and eat a little of the food Maya made for us before climbing into the truck to continue our journey.

"Are you warm enough?" our mother asks and the three of us answer in unison, "We're fine."

I pull my coat over my head and once more fall asleep.

Father drives for several hours before he pulls off the road to find somewhere to park for the night. We have something to eat and I help make us a warm drink, before we get ready to sleep in the truck. We are a little cramped but Father assures us that it is just for one night. Although I want to sleep, for some reason I just can't. My thoughts go round and round, I am scared of what might happen to us in England. Well, we have to get there first. Father said it would take just a couple of days and we should look at it as going on holiday and having an exciting adventure. Hmm, maybe.

When we wake up the next morning the sun is shining and I should be happy. Happy to be with my family, and yes, part of me is. It is just that I am so scared about England. I keep telling myself, it will be all right, I will be with my family. Father loves England and he keeps telling us that we will love it too.

Another day squashed between my brother and sister, and another and another. One day just rolls into another, the boredom is crushing. I am not even taking any interest in my baby brother Sami. I just sit with my arms folded and coat over my head.

I don't answer when anyone speaks to me. Sayid pokes me in the ribs to wake me up when Mother or Father talk to me. I am there just wallowing in self-pity. We do not need to leave, we have money, property, Father said so himself.

Will this journey ever end? Father said we would only have to sleep one night in the truck. I have lost count how many nights it has been. Mother puts on a brave face and says "The drive will soon be over, won't it Nizar?"

Father replies, "It should have been over days ago, I must have miscalculated somehow. I have always flown to Athens when I have visited my agent in Greece. He has arranged for us to collect our new passports at Idomeni."

He added, "I need to look at my properties in Greece so that if I need to sell any of them I will know which ones to put on the market".

So we have to collect more passports. Father feels the ones we have are not good enough should we need to show them to board the ferry to England. When Father went to England he went by plane and he had an English passport. He knows nothing about travelling by sea, only what he has read.

I am making him so wrong. He should have had everything ready, so that we do not have to travel so far in this truck. We have to travel by road as my mother is unable to go by plane due to her recent operation.

Sayid digs me in the ribs and shouts, "The sea, I can see the sea, listen to the sea gulls squawk". He was fast asleep when we crossed the narrow strait from mainland Turkey into Istanbul.

Father parks the truck and starts to tell us what happens next. "We will drive to the refugee camp called Idomeni to collect our new passports. I have already paid some of the money for them. Then I will go to see my agent and make appointments to view my properties. We can then do some sightseeing before we drive to Calais where we catch the ferry to England. When we arrive in Dover I will just need to contact Ken and we will spend our first few nights with him and his family.

"We will not have too far to drive from Dover. Ken and Doreen his wife live with their three children in Christchurch which is in what is called the New

Forest. Ponies run wild in the New Forest and they take precedence over humans and vehicles. We can camp in the New Forest too."

We arrive at Idomeni. It all looks so chaotic, untidy and crowded. It seems like everyone is crowding around our truck. No one is smiling; they are just staring and saying nothing.

Father gets out of the truck and approaches the group of people. After introducing himself he asks where he can find Mr Ben Joseph. The group starts to laugh in a cruel sort of way. "He's gone; he'll be back in a couple of weeks ... maybe."

Not talking to anyone in particular Father says, "But he told me to meet him here!"
One man responds, "You and 20 others ... I bet you have paid him money too?" Father nods and the man says, "Well, I suppose we ought to find you somewhere to park."

"Well, if he is not here we'll go and do a little sightseeing and come back in a couple of days."

"Suit yourselves."

Father gets back into the truck smiling and saying thank you to the group, "I'll be back in a couple of days," and with a wave of his hand we drive out through the entrance again.

We only go a few hundred yards outside the camp when Father stops the truck and curls up with his elbows resting on the steering wheel, head in his hands.

He spends five minutes like this before straightening up and saying, "Right, this is the plan. I am sure I saw signs to a campsite not far away. We'll go there, pay to pitch our tent for a couple of nights and I can visit my agent tomorrow. Maybe he knows where Mr. Ben Joseph is. Then we'll come back here to see if he has returned in a day or so."

Mother is holding baby Sami in one arm and puts her other arm across Father's shoulders. She speaks somewhat anxiously, "It will be all right, won't it?"

"Yes of course, everything will be fine. I will telephone Ken to give him an update of our journey so far."

It does not take us long to reach the campsite. We are lucky; it seems there has been a cancellation so we can take that space. With a map of the complex in hand Father drives us to our allotted pitch. Now the fun begins as we start to erect the tent. Father had bought the tent brand new two weeks before we left because he thought the old one had become worn out. There are so many pieces. Father exasperatedly asks, "Which bit goes where?"

"I think maybe you should read the directions, dear," Mother laughs.

Long bendy pieces of plastic are threaded into tubes stitched into the fabric. Wow! Like magic a tent appears. We can attach ropes to hold it in place or add

further pieces of fabric and plastic to make separate rooms. Although this takes time Father thinks it a good idea to have the tent erected with all the various compartments.

Mother and I go in search of some food that we don't have to cook so we can just snuggle down in our sleeping bags for a well-earned rest.

We buy chicken and noodles, bread, fresh fruit and milk for hot drinks before bed. Of course this depends on whether or not Father has put the cooker together.

The baby's buggy makes a good shopping trolley so we have no bags to carry and soon make it back to our tent which, to our surprise, is completely erected. Mattresses and sleeping bags are all laid out too. "Rosarita was a great help making the beds," my father says. It all looks very cosy.

"Who's for food?" Mother asks. "Yes please," we all say at once. " Get plates and cutlery from the trailer then and sit at the table and eat."

After supper we go in search of the showers. It is only afterwards, when I am curled up in my sleeping bag trying to go to sleep that it hit me. We are not on holiday; we have left our home to go to England, that country my father loves. Sleep finally comes.

In the morning Father calls Ken and we find where the bank is so Father can check his bank account and withdraw money. He puts his arm around Mother and gives her a hug saying, "We will be fine. Who's for an ice cream?" Even I say, "Yes".

Decisions, decisions, what flavour shall I have? Double chocolate or vanilla. I'll have both. We continue walking slowly, stopping to look in various shop windows.

"Well, what are we going to do for the rest of the day?" Mother asks. Father says, "We could go back to the camp site and see what activities are available." Sayid cries excitedly, "Yes, let's." Everyone else agrees, so we collect the information on what is happening today and return to our tent.

Although we have not done very much we are all very tired, so we decide we will have an hour's sleep and then do some exploring and go for a swim in the camp pool. The next day we visit the refugee camp. No Mr Ben Joseph.

Back at the tent Father says that "We can stay in this spot for two weeks, so let's make a holiday of it. None of us like going to the refugee camp so I'll go on my own every day." Everyone agrees so he pays for two weeks to pitch on this plot. For the next 10 days he visits the refugee camp every day and still no Mr. Ben Joseph. Father's agent has no idea where Mr. Ben Joseph might be.

After he has paid for the two week stay Father says, "There is just one thing. We must take care of your mother, I know that she has recovered well from the difficult birth of Sami, and the surgery involved but she still needs rest. Especially as she is still breast feeding Sami."

"I am fine," Mother says, "you worry too much. I will rest when I need to, I promise."

Mother, Sayid and I visit reception and collect tourist information on what there is to see, where to go and what to do on our holiday. Father and Rosarita meet us there and we catch a bus into town.

We go exploring in the town on a shopping spree for holiday clothes. I find a gorgeous sun hat which Mother calls my rainbow hat as it has various coloured ribbons which drape down my back. Father has made arrangements with his agent to visit some of his properties and he promises he will not be long. We were all so pleased to see him return especially as he thinks he can sell a couple of the properties locally for a substantial profit.

One day we take a boat trip, it is quite windy so I pull my hat as far down on my head as it would go and then put both hands on top of my head to make sure it doesn't blow away.

Almost every day I swim in the camp pool and play games with other children on the camp site. Sometimes we all go swimming and Mother would read a book or sit playing with Sami.

She was walking faster and further each day having organised an exercise schedule for herself. Often I would accompany her on these walks around the campsite and we would talk.

Occasionally Father would drive us a little way along the coast just to look at the scenery, not so very different from home. Mother would mostly take this opportunity to have a nap.

The only meal we cook is breakfast, and we all help with this, even little Rosarita, still clutching her stuffed dog. All our other meals we eat in restaurants. This means no one has to prepare any food. We have an amazing time and I am so very pleased that we have this holiday as it gives me something to cling on to in the days, weeks and months to come.

The time comes when we know we can only stay where we are for two more nights because the campsite is fully booked. Father has become friends with the site owner, Frank Langous, and he is going to see if he can find some way for us to stay on the site. Everything is going to be fine.

So the plan for tomorrow is that we start to pack up ready to leave the day after, that is if Frank cannot find us anywhere to move our tent to.

Father says, "Let's go and eat now, and stop thinking about tomorrow." I remember the delicious chocolate gateau which had fresh cream and ice cream along with the melted chocolate.

Back at the campsite we get ready for bed. I give Mother and Father a hug, plant a kiss on Sami's head and go into my part of the tent. Rosarita and Sayid are already fast asleep. I hear Mother say, "I should not have eaten all that cake, delicious though it was. It is giving me a little indigestion. Father replies, "Would you like me to get you anything?"

"No, I'll be fine. I will just feed Sami and then go to sleep. Thank you, Nizar, for this lovely holiday. I am sure it has helped the children to accept going to England. It will be alright in England, won't it?

"Of course it will. Good night, dear."

The next day is a beautiful sunny morning. For the past few days I've been woken by Sami crying for his breakfast but not today. I pull back the flap of the tent that separates my room and my parents. I look into their room and Mother is laying on her side, she looks strange.

I try to wake her but she doesn't respond so I call Father. When he sees her he pushes me out of the way saying, "Quick, go and get help." Father pulls back Mother's sleeping bag, lifts baby Sami up and puts him in his crib, then he turns Mother onto her back and starts to push on her chest and blow into her mouth. I run from the tent screaming, "Help, Help", I run along the gravelled path barefoot, and do not feel anything. "Please , please help, my mother is sick."

Other campers come to help; one is a nurse and she tries to revive Sami while a man helps my father. In a little while an ambulance arrives and my mother is put on to a trolley while Sami is wrapped in a shawl. Father gets into the ambulance and Frank tells him not to worry, he'll take care of us. Just give us a call and let us know what is happening.

The three of us just stand still as the doors of the ambulance are slammed shut and speed out of the campsite. Frank says, "Well! That was a bit of a shock. Our hospital is so good and not far away. Come on, let's get you some breakfast".

I am not feeling hungry but I do try to eat some toast. Rosarita sits clutching her dog and asks, "When will Father and Mother be back?" Frank says, "As soon as they can. Your father is going to call me with any news. Why don't you go for a walk with Martine? I know you could help her clean out the stables. I know you love horses. I will let you know what's happening as soon as I hear from your father."

It is well into the afternoon before we hear anything from my father. Frank finds us at the stables and tells us Father is on his way back here. I ask, "How's my

mother and baby brother?" Frank responds rather sheepishly, "Your father will tell you when he gets here. Come along now, dinner is ready. You have all worked so hard today, you must all be hungry?"

My father finds us eating dinner; Frank asks him to sit down and eat. Father says he is not hungry. I can't wait any longer and burst out, "How about Mother and Sami?"

My father starts to cry. He blurts out, "They are both dead".

Frank takes over, "There will have to be an inquest as to what happened and a post-mortem to find out why it happened. The medics think that your mother had a heart attack and rolled onto Sami and suffocated him."

We all start to cry, this is just not real and I am having a nightmare. I will wake up in the morning and everything will be fine. If only that were true.

Frank asks my father, "Did the authorities tell you when you will be contacted?"

Father says, "We will be contacted in a couple of days and we will all be interviewed. I think they will be asking you questions too."

Frank says he needs to go to his office and will be back soon. I put my head in my hands and just cry. Nothing will ever be the same again. What is going to happen to us?

Frank returns and says, "I have managed to change some of the plots around so you will be able to stay where you are for another week."

That is one problem solved but I am just going around in a dream. I make sure my brother and sister shower, clean their teeth and change their clothes. Somehow I learn to use a washing machine, I never had to do any washing before. Maya always took care of that.

Father sits with his head in his hands moaning to himself, "Why did I not see there was a problem, that she was unwell? I've looked after 100's of people with her condition and they recovered from a heart attack. This is all my fault."

Just then a man puts his head into the tent and asks for Father. The man shows Father his identification and asks us all to accompany him to reception as we are to be asked some questions. He has a vehicle outside so we don't need to walk.

Rosarita, Sayid and I are taken to one room at the back of Frank's office and my father is taken to another. We enter this room where a lady and gentleman are sitting behind a desk with a pile of papers in front of them. The lady asks us to sit down and if we would like something to drink. We say no thank you together.

Then she says she is sorry about the deaths of my mother and baby brother but she needs to ask us some questions about our mother. She also says that if we don't understand the question, please say so. We will try to be as brief as possible. We want to know about your family and how you came to be in Greece.

They ask where we live, about our parents, were there any problems, did my parents argue, she goes on and on while we answer as best as we can. We describe what we did on Mother's last day including what we remember her eating and drinking. At last the interview is over, we are thanked and are taken to our father. The officer that drove us here is waiting to drive us back to our tent. While driving us back he tells us that our statements will be examined and will be taken to court along with the findings of the post-mortem in two days time. He also says we should be there at 10am.

Frank comes to court with us. We listen to the judge outlining what had happened. From the findings of the post mortem Mother had had a heart attack, possibly caused by a blood clot from the operation when she had Sami, and that Sami was suffocated. The judge was sympathetic and said that Mother's and baby Sami's bodies could now be taken by an undertaker and arrangements made to have them buried.

Mr and Mrs Langos are such a tower of strength. They organise everything for my mother's funeral. The cost of the funeral is not a problem, thankfully

Father has plenty of money in the bank but he has gone to pieces. He just stares into space, and we have to ask him the same question over and over.

My mother and brother are buried in a lovely spot overlooking the sea. None of us want to leave the graveside. It all seems so final. I need you, Mother. Please, please what am I to do?

Frank has tried to find us another plot so that we can stay on the campsite but to no avail. He suggests we camp at the refugee site until we get our passports adding, "We can take care of your truck and trailer until you are ready to leave. When I have a spare plot I can come and collect you but I hope you'll be in England before that."

Surely Mr Ben Joseph will be back now?

We just take the middle part of the tent and a few possessions. The rest of our stuff goes into the trailer and Father drives it to reception. I have the thought, this is not real, it's is a horror story, I am dreaming, dreaming!

But it's not a dream. Frank drives us to the refugee camp and helps us put up our tent. He says, "It's not going to be for long, Nizar, you should soon get your passports and we will keep in touch". With a wave he drives out onto the road. What now?

Father sits with his head in his hands. I ask, "We should go and look around, so we know where the toilets are and where we can get water?"

Reluctantly he gets up and we all go to find out where we can wash and get drinking water. On our way back to our tent Father asks a group of men if Mr Ben Joseph has been back.

The response was very vague, "Haven't seen him, shouldn't be long now though. Fancy a game of cards?" Father says, "No thanks" and we go back to our tent where we have something to eat, and get ready for bed. Sayid asks if we can keep the light on. Father nods, "For a little while".

Just before I go to bed Father says to me, "We shouldn't have to stay here long, Rubina. It is so hard without Mother. Go to sleep now, I won't be very long, I am just going for a walk. Keep the light on if you want to."

I did not hear him come back but the next morning he was stretched out on his bed holding a bottle of whisky which he continued to drink throughout the day. I was able to buy us some food with a little of the money that I had. Father did not want any food, just another bottle of whisky.

Frank comes to visit, but cannot take us back to his campsite. He seems at a loss as to what to say to my father. Weeks pass, the weather becomes very cold and it seems to rain non-stop.

Father takes to drinking heavily. We were lucky when the authorities come around the site to look for children that are on their own. They look into the tent and see my Father asleep and walk away. Time drags. What am I to do?

I had better see if I can get some food. I bend over to put on my boots and Father wakes up. He sees my gold necklace and grabs it, yanking it from my neck. I try to pull it from his hand but he is too strong for me. "No, no, Father, it is all I have left from Mother." He also takes my winter coat pushing me away and goes to see the men who sell him whisky.

I see they greet him warmly as he tries to sell my locket and coat. I can hear him shouting. The men take him a little way from our tent so I can't hear what is being said. Later I am told what happened.

Apparently it went something like this; "Look Nizar, we are no longer going to supply you with whisky. We are sorry for the loss of your wife and baby but you have three other children to care for. They have lost their mother too. Rubina is doing her best but she is still a child in many ways. Look what you are trying to sell, your daughter's coat, what's next?"

You are a doctor, what would you tell relatives when they lose a loved one?"

"It was my fault she died; I should have recognized the signs."

"That may be but you cannot turn the clock back, you can only go forward. Doctor, heal yourself. We will do all we can to help you. But no more drink. Let's go to my tent. We are getting soaked out here."

Apparently the conversation continued something like this, "Look Nizar, if you don't shape up we are going to have to report you, and your children will be taken away. Just think on that, your wife would not want that now would she?"

I search in my rucksack for the money I have hidden in a rolled up sock. I tip the contents of my rucksack onto my bed. I search but the money is nowhere to be found. I tip the bag upside down; nothing.

The meagre money I had is gone; I know where - to buy father's whisky. That is why he lies there in a drunken stupor. I cannot blame him; he misses my mother so much. We all miss her but I have no other choice now. I have to look after Sayid and Rosarita because Father is not really here. I'll have to go to the soup kitchen to get food. I pull on my boots and put on my waterproof, looking at Sayid and Rosarita, "Promise me that you'll stay in bed till I get back with some food?" They nod and say "Yes".

I loosen the flap on the tent and step out into the rain. The ground is nothing but mud. I slip and grab the tent pole for support. Fortunately the pole stays upright. Gingerly I step into this quagmire. At last, when I reached the soup kitchen the queue for food is very long. I am wet, cold and hungry. I started thinking of Mother, as if I am having a conversation with her. In my mind I ask, "Why did you have to die? You made everything bearable when you were here. What am I to do? Father is drunk all the time, we have no money, nothing to barter with, what can I do? It is pouring with rain and I am so cold, hungry and wet, why is the queue not moving?" Eventually, after several hours, I get into the large tent where the food is served. There are only three people in front and ... there is no food!

The aid worker says, "Nothing left, it's all gone."

I burst into tears and the aid worker tells me, "I can't magic food and drink out of thin air, get here early tomorrow". I turn away crying and suddenly feel an arm go gently across my shoulders. I turn again and am hugged by the lady behind me. I bury my wet face into her chest. We walk out of the food tent together in silence supporting each other.

I don't know what to do. I walk with the lady, not knowing where we are going. Suddenly through my tears I can see a crowd gathering at the camp entrance. "What's going on?" I ask a woman who comes away carrying two loaves of bread. "It's the bread man. He brings us bread that he can't sell."

My new companion and I quicken our pace towards the van parked at the entrance to the camp. I see other people come away with loaves of bread, so I desperately, silently scream, "Please, please let there be one for me!"

Somehow the crowd has shrunk and we are at the front. The baker gives us a loaf and says, "Here you are, this is the last large loaf I have."

I clutch his hand and started kissing it, "Thank you, thank you."

"Just a minute", the baker looks in his van and came out with a jam cake which he gives to me. "Here you are. I come every day at about this time to give away what is not sold in my shop. Tomorrow is Saturday so if you want bread tomorrow make sure you are here early as I do not come on Sundays."

I cover the bread and cake with my waterproof and thank the baker again turning to the lady, "Thank you so much for being so kind and I do not even know your name. Mine is Rubina."

She replies, "I'm Amina."

This lady seems so kind. I break a piece of the bread and give it to Amina saying, "Why don't you come back to our tent for a while?" The rain has stopped so Amina collects a few pieces of dry cardboard and follows me. I go into the tent and sit on my bed sharing out the bread and cake. Amina, puts down the cardboard on the floor and sits next to me.

After a few minutes I get up and go and talk with a woman who is just leaving a crowd of people at the entrance. Apparently a lot of the men want to walk about 6 kilometres across farmland and woods to force their way across the border. There seems to be some agreement because the crowd breaks up and I hear someone say "OK, 10am tomorrow". Amina comes with me to tell Father and he agrees we should try it.

At about 10am we see lots of people moving towards the camp entrance, many of them carrying bags of various kinds, pushing or pulling little carts loaded with their belongings.

We join them but we don't take anything with us. It is raining again and I don't see Amina. We walk slowly with the crowd, Father holding Rosarita's hand, she holds Sayid's hand and he holds mine.

The crowd turns off the track outside the camp and we start to cross fields. Slipping and sliding in the mud makes walking hard work but fortunately none of us fall down. After what seems like hours we come to a stop. We hear there's a stream up ahead and it's full with all the recent rain.

In the confusion I see Amina. She looks lost but I am so pleased to see her and she seems pleased to see us. She tells us about the river and says she's scared to cross. Father says, "We'll have a look and you can come with us. It may not be as bad as you think."

We get to the river bank and it does not look inviting. It's dirty, fast flowing and probably icy cold. Still, people are wading across. I watch one boy about Sayid's size and the water almost covers him but someone puts an arm under him and keeps his head above water. He looks very cold when he reaches the far bank.

I notice some people abandoning their baggage before they cross the river while others try to take it with them. Most of them lose it but everyone is getting across.

Amina is scared, she says she cannot cross, and is too afraid to try. I reach for her hand, look into her eyes and tell her I know she can do it. Our family all take deep breaths and focus on the far bank, probably about 5 metres away. We all step into the cold water together, I'm holding Amina's hand on one side and Sayid's hand on the other side. Father has Rosarita on his shoulders and she clutches her bedraggled stuffed dog. The water is dirty, cold and deep enough to come up to Sayid's chin. But we all make it!

We take a few minutes to catch our breath and hear noises coming from nearby woods. Looking towards the woods to our right we see police on horses coming quickly in our direction. Amina calls me to follow her towards the woods in front of us when suddenly this big black horse is between Amina and me. I hear a scream and I know Amina is being beaten. I try to stop it by grabbing the rider on the horse by the foot but he kicks me away. I don't see what happens to Amina.

Father has managed to hide Sayid and Rosarita in the woods so he comes to find me. We seem to be hiding there for hours but it is too dangerous to move. We are wet, cold and hungry and there is nothing we can do about it.

Father says, "I don't see any point in staying at Idomeni so we should go to the camp they call the Jungle. At least it'll be nearer to England. It's likely to be several days travel but I don't see anything else for it so this is what we'll do. We will go back to Idomeni the way we came, it does mean crossing that stream again in the dark but we've done it once so the next time isn't so bad. We'll get everything together that we want to take with us, collect our truck and trailer from Frank. We can go and visit Mother's grave and I will visit my agent to give him instructions what to do if he is unable to contact me."

I ask, "What about Amina?"

Father replies, "We have already looked and looked for her. She may have gone back to the camp. We'll collect the truck and trailer from Frank, then once it's all loaded we'll take another look around the camp before we leave."

As dusk approaches we slowly come out of the wood and find there's nobody to be seen. The stream is only a few hundred metres away but Father wants to cross it where we crossed originally. He says that way we can be reasonably sure of a safe crossing.

Following the stream in the growing darkness is easy enough, what bothers me is that I'm going to get wet and cold again. Eventually we find the crossing place and slide down into the water, Father carrying Rosarita with her stuffed dog on his shoulders once more and holding Sayid's hand while Sayid holds mine.

Father stumbles as we reach the far bank and tips Rosarita into the water. She howls and won't shut up. Up on the bank Father tells her he's sorry and kindly asks her to stop crying. She comes to me and puts her face into my soaking clothes, then I realise that she has lost her stuffed dog. That's what she is upset about.

It is a slow walk back to the camp. I never thought I'd be so pleased to see that disgusting place and I'm even more pleased to see our tent has been untouched. On the way in we saw several devastated places where people's tents have been ransacked in their absence.

Father says, "Rubina, help Rosarita and Sayid get into dry clothes please. It doesn't matter that they are not clean ones. You do the same. I'm going to fetch water for tea before we go to sleep."

He goes off and I get my brother and sister out of their wet, dirty clothes. They are into bed by the time Father comes back so while he makes tea I get changed too. With the tea he produces a packet of biscuits and says, "I'm sorry it's all I could scrounge."

We all go to sleep and when we wake in the morning the sun is shining brilliantly. Another cup of tea and we all go off unwashed to collect our truck and trailer. Frank and Martine are really glad to see us, they've heard terrible stories about the events of yesterday.

Father tells them of our plans and Frank says, "It's probably a good idea. The authorities have wanted to close Idomeni for some time now. This will give them the excuse they want."

Frank and Martine agree to look after Mother and Sami's grave until we can come back to make other arrangements. Father is really grateful for the help they have given us and doesn't know what to say. That's a first.

Back in the camp we pack the trailer really quickly, we all want to be away from here. We visit Frank and Martine again and say goodbye, with hugs all round.

Driving down the road Father spots a flower stall. He buys a large bunch of the flowers Mother liked and we go to their grave. We stand with our arms around each other tears streaming down our faces.

"We need to leave," Father says. "Dry your eyes and we will be off."

It takes us 7 days to reach Calais. We go and visit the Jungle first where Father enquires after Mr. Ben Joseph. No news of him so no passports.

We look around the camp where we are going to stay. Father talks to lots of people to gather information on how to get to England.

At the Jungle we learn that we have to take calculated chances to get to England. One of the things we hadn't considered was sea-sickness but Father soon solves that difficulty by buying tablets to take as soon as we've secured a ride.

Father talks to some officials and shows them our papers. They are not good enough, so we can't just take the truck and trailer onto the ferry and go that way. Father seems to go round and round in circles trying to work out how we can travel. We walk towards the docks and watch the vehicles drive onto the ferry.

For the first time our family has to sleep apart. Father is on his own sleeping in a big polythene tunnel with other men. I sleep with Rosarita and Sayid in a similar tunnel in a part of the camp called Jules Ferry. This is where all the females and children are kept safe.

We continue like this, attempting to get lifts on lorries during the day and sleeping in these tunnels for more than two weeks. One night I am just falling asleep when I sense someone is looking at me. It takes me a few minutes to realise it is Amina. I am so pleased to see her. We just hug each other silently. She's sleeping just a few spaces away from me and it is comforting to know that she has made it this far too.

Next morning we go to see Father for breakfast. He is so pleased to see Amina. Father tells her, "We've had no luck in getting on a lorry. But not to worry, I feel we'll have a ride tonight and you can come with us, Amina, I will pay for you."

About sunset we meet the driver of a lorry carrying vegetables who agrees to take us. He knows it is a risk for him but he is prepared to take that riskas his family needs the money. Father hands him some money and says he will receive more if we are undetected on the crossing to Dover. Father then asks the driver to exchange some Euros for British pounds so that we have some usable money in England. We all climb in the back of the lorry and the driver shows us where to hide ourselves. We take our sickness pills and make ourselves as comfortable as possible.

The driver says, "Do not leave your hiding place until I come and get you." He's very firm about this and repeats the instruction several times. "I have never taken refugees in my lorry before. This is a big risk for me, but my family needs the money."

The lorry joins the queue to board the ferry and we hear dogs barking outside. The back doors open and we see the beams from the torches being shone into the lorry. Amina clutches my hand, we are both frightened. The doors close again and the truck rolls on to the ferry. We are in darkness. The smell from the vegetables is strong. I feel sick.

Soon the ferry starts to move and I hold my breath, praying for a smooth crossing and that no one will be sick.

It is a smooth crossing so none of us are sick. We dock in Dover and feel the bumps in the ramps as the lorry slowly drives off the ferry. The lorry stops and more lights shine into the lorry, more dogs bark, but we remain quiet and undetected. We are to stay in our hiding place until the driver tells us it is safe to come out, I hope that it will not take too long before we can stand up. I feel quite strange, then I realize that none of us have had anything to drink for about 6 hours.

The lorry drives for what seems like hours until the back doors swing open, the darkness has changed to light and at last we are able to stand up. The driver helps us down from the lorry as we are all so stiff. England, we've made it! I never thought I would say I am pleased to be in England.

The driver and Father exchange more money, then the driver says, "I must be off now. Walk across that field and you'll come to another road, turn right and round the corner is a cafe. I'm not doing this again, too much for me. Good Luck" and he has gone.

Father explains where we are and adds, "We'll go to the cafe and hopefully I can make a phone call and give Ken directions on how to find us". We start walking slowly across the field. This helps loosen up our joints. I am still so stiff from our journey. The sun is just coming up, it all looks so pretty. Very different from the scenery back home.

We arrive at the cafe and we are all so thirsty and hungry, Father asks for a full English breakfast whatever that is for each of us, along with orange juice and a jug of water. Wow, when it comes, the plates are loaded with eggs, sausages, bacon, mushrooms, tomatoes and baked beans. We are all so very hungry, that we all eat our food quickly. As we eat I see Father looking round and realise he's looking for a telephone. He doesn't see one so he asks the waitress if there is a phone he can use. She points him to a corner so after he has finished eating he goes over to the corner to make the phone call. He finds the phone is a coin in the slot machine so he has to go to the counter to get change.

When he comes back he explains, "Ken will be with us as soon as he can but it will take some time, a couple of hours at least. He has given me a description of his vehicle so we just have to wait."

Breakfast over, I realize I am very tired but there is nowhere to sleep. I ask Father if I can go outside and to my surprise he says no. We have nothing to do except sit here. Rosarita is playing with her dog. I start to tease her and Father gives me one of his looks which means 'Stop It'. He says that we should all go for a short walk, keeping the car park of the cafe in view. So we walk around and around. It's a dry day so we sit on the grass and go to sleep.

It is early afternoon when Ken arrives. Father is so pleased to see him and introduces us all before we climb into his 7-seater car and we set off for Christchurch. Ken has thoughtfully brought us drinks and snacks to eat during our journey and books and games that his children play with when they are travelling, never mind that they are all in English.

The motion of the car just sends me to sleep. I rest my head on Amina's shoulder and the next thing I remember is that we are arriving at Ken's house in the late afternoon. His wife and children greet us warmly.

It's time for their evening meal which they share with us, shepherd's pie and it is served with vegetables. Christine, one of Ken's children tells us the vegetables are grown in their own garden.

After our meal we are shown up to our bedrooms. Doreen says, "Please use this house as your home. If you need anything just ask". I look at my bedroom from the door. It is beautiful, matching curtains and bedspread, my own shower. Doreen takes Rosarita and Amina into the next room while I take off my clothes step into the shower. The shower feels cold to my feet but it is not a concrete floor. I wash my hair and just let the warm water run down my back, enjoying the sensation. I am so glad the journey is over.

Climbing out of the shower I find beautiful white fluffy towels on the bed to dry myself with. Rosarita comes into the room, she wants to sleep with me and that is fine. I pull back the bedspread and climb into a real bed with beautiful cotton sheets. I lay down and my head sinks into a fluffy pillow. I feel so happy and blessed I start to cry. Rosarita wants to know why! I am just so happy.

The next day cars start arriving. Ken has apparently told the other people he and Father trained with in medical school and now they are here to greet us. After all the introductions a man called David became the spokesperson; "You must listen to your doctors. We cannot escape the fact that you are illegal immigrant refugees. We have all written letters for you when you are interviewed by the various authorities and we don't expect the process to take more than a couple of months. We're desperately short of people in your field.

"In the meantime you need time to recuperate from all that you have endured. Please feel free to spend time with any one of us and treat our homes as yours. We also insist that you take this gift. It is a small token and thanks for all you did for each one of us when we trained. You taught us, fed us, and had fun with us. So this money is a way of saying thank you for all you did for us. Besides, we thought you might need some ready cash. Nizar, through you we have become better people which means we are better at dealing with life."

There were a lot of tears and hugs that day. I also came to see what a very special father I have. Richard offers to take Amina to her uncle in a place called Leicester as she is so anxious to see him. The bonds of friendship between us are so strong we will always be part of each other's lives however far apart we live. We cry and hug and she is gone. My wonderful friend and sister Amina.

Dean Robinson

I am a south London-born male of West Indian descent who in primary school discovered a penchant for poetry and prose. Although my childhood was spent dreaming about writing, it wasn't until the age of 32 that I picked up a pen and took myself seriously.

That's when I decided to do a creative writing degree at Birkbeck University. There, under the tutelage of some well-known and published writers, I was able to learn the basics of the craft, and since then I've been trying to develop my voice.

'Holding On' is a story born from an observation of the plight and struggle of our friends in the refugee crisis. It's an ode to their tenacity and courage, as well as a testament to every one of us who needs encouragement to hold onto the dreams that nourish and enliven the soul.

Holding On

(Photo credit: Cristian Palmer, unspash.com)

My lungs hold onto the last gasp of air that I had taken up there on the water's surface. My hands are tense, fingers outstretched reaching upwards towards the vessel from which I fell. I watch as it passes overhead and the terror begins to build somewhere deep inside me as I realise something: I am alone.

Is this panic? I can't feel my clothes, though they must be clinging to my sinking torso; can't feel my trousers; can't even feel my black leather shoes that I bought at home in Aleppo before all the fighting started. All I feel is this air that I am fighting to hold on to.

You know, the funny thing is that it seems to be fighting back. It pounds onto the inside of my chest, like a demon crying to break free from hell. Hell because it burns inside me, so much so that I become privy to something else, a vague sensation of wetness, which is strange considering it's all around me. It's everything that I can see. And, with every eternal second that passes, my thoracic temperature rises until I feel as if I'm going to implode into lava, brimstone and damnation. Water is the only remedy, the only thing that can satisfy the flames.

My hands instinctively move to my mouth, covering it, as if holding onto the gas inside it will ensure my safety. But then I feel my body start to shake. I can't control the convulsing fits, the coughing, as my reptilian brain fights to contain this ancient elixir.

Flailing now, reaching for the sky even though I am sinking faster and faster to what must be the seabed, totally unable to see that every resistance is one of futility. It's too late. I can't do it. I have to open up, to breathe in the air that I know isn't there.

In rushes the seawater and there's a hope that this is what I need to end the misery, but then the inevitable choking begins. This is the struggle, the real horror. The kicking and reaching and grabbing at water molecules that just glide through my every grasp. It doesn't take long for the tremors to slow, to eventually stop, for the flailing to cease.

Everything slows down.

I can't move my body anymore and it doesn't matter because somewhere deep inside me knows that there is no need, not anymore.

For some reason everything turns on. Light burns bright from unknown sources. I can hear whispers, chattering and screams, both close and yet far away. I feel like I can smell the water that surrounds me. But isn't that ridiculous? It smells of mum's tabouleh. The way it was presented to us with the utmost precision and with not a drop of oil or sauce around the edges of the plate. The strobe of sunlight beams onto the dining table trying to rejuvenate a bunch of lilies that hang from a vase with tips tinged with rust.

*   *   *

The clock read five pm. A mild anxiety grew inside me at the thought of Hassan waiting for me to finish so that we could carry on with our game of football. I fought to keep the anxiety at bay but rushed my lunch. I spooned the vegetables into my mouth with pieces of bread and washed it down with water from a glass that shook in my hands.

"Hold on Khalif, don't inhale your food," said mum as she so quietly sat beside me. Her eyes were saying something, something that I hadn't developed the maturity to understand yet. Hope. She rubbed my back and regarded me with healing eyes.

"Oh, and have you been writing in your journal? You must always write, Khalif, so that when you turn into a man you can understand what it is to be a boy, for one day you too will have children. You must know how to relate to them." I nodded stuffing myself with the last of the tabouleh.

"I'm finished, mum. Can I go out now?" The food still moved around in my mouth while I spoke. She smiled with a defeated exhalation and then nodded. I got up from my seat in such haste that the glass of water I'd been drinking fell over and spilled onto her brown shawl. Hope turned to helplessness. She sprang up from her chair with hands raised towards heaven, standing there like a statue watching the wetness run down the material on her legs.

"Khalif! You're always in such a rush. You know that now is not the time to be wasting water!"

"Sorry, mother."

I was confused to see more wetness leaking from her eyes before her hand covered her mouth and she turned away from me.

"Sorry mother!" Her gaze was fixed onto the spillage and she seemed to break into a chuckle.

"It's ok, my little angel," she said as she stroked my hair. "You can go out now. Hassan is waiting for you, isn't he?"

I nodded, smiled and left the room.

"What took you so long, little brother?" said Hassan, focused on the tennis ball that he was throwing up against a wall and catching the rebound.

"Nothing. I just finished eating... and stop calling me that. You're only six months older than me."

He laughed into the palm of his hand. The ball bounced on the floor and he controlled it with his feet.

"Today, little brother, we will learn about soccer." I rolled my eyes to the blue cloudless sky and shook my head. I stood with my arms akimbo waiting for his monologue to come to an end. He loved the sound of his own voice.

"You see, little brother, the British are obsessed with the art of ball control," he said rolling the ball onto his foot to play with it like a hackey sack. I saw the ball move from his left foot to his right, and then up he kicked it to his left knee and then to right knee before it landed on the floor as he covered it with the sole of his foot. Then he passed it to me.

"Now you try."

I rolled the ball onto the top of my foot. I thought I had it balanced just right but when I tried to lift it, it just rolled off. This happened five times before Hassan said that I should try picking the ball up and dropping it onto my foot so that I could at least get started. He was amazed at my inability to kick the ball from one foot to another.

We spent all day out there, underneath the sun, my mother coming out routinely to offer us more water. We were so engrossed in play that we

96

didn't even notice. When at last we sat down to get our breath back, I called to my mum asking for more water. Her face poked out of a window. "I'm so sorry, boys. I'll have to go down to the shop and get some more.

"Oh no, Mrs Eliyahi. It's fine. We'll go and get some for you."

"Oh Hassan, thank you. That would be so helpful. When you come back, make sure that you stay for dinner."
At the shop I remember the long queue.

"What is everyone queuing for?" Hassan asked one of the locals.

Someone replied "Meat and vegetables, just the normal everyday staples that we live on from day to day."

The man chuckled. "Why would you have heard about this? If I were your age, I wouldn't be concerned about this either." His eyes were round, innocent and they were pointing at me.

I shrugged my shoulders. He took in a deep breath and sighed. "A number of farms have had to close down this year due to the drought. We're standing in this long line because there are no longer shops filled with all of the meat and vegetables that we are used to."

"So, what must we do?" I said.

"Right," said the man. "What must we do?"

*   *   *

There is nothing I can do. Drifting downwards, faint images of indistinguishable objects pass me by. Above my head it looks like a school of fish travel in unison in the shape of a V. Not one of them fall out of formation as they dart left and right, up and down. In their movements there is something unspeakably familiar. And somewhere in the distant darkness familiar voices permeate this space.

*   *   *

"There is no real need to wait any longer, is there Amala?" Khalif will be eleven soon. He is smart for his age and he will make a good husband one day."

"And Larissa is a beautiful young girl. One day she will be a woman who will use her beauty and intelligence to support and respect her husband."

"That's just it, sister. I fear for her future, their future. Life here is growing arid and stale. We have gone from running out of water to running out of patience. There was a fight that broke out in the market-place today and twelve people were injured needlessly."

My aunt called my mother with that reassuring tone. "Amala," "This was due to happen. Our government is in ruins and the people are not convinced that there is a sure and clear future. It's completely out of our hands."

"And what about our economic situation? Amir acts as though everything is ok with work, but rumours suggest that they are making cuts at the factory. Even though he is a manager, that might not be enough to secure his position."

"Sister, please! It isn't worth worrying about things that we have no control over at the present."

"That's easy to say when you don't have any dependents to worry about. If anything happened to Khalif I'd never be able to live with myself."

"That's not fair, Amala. I have been trying to conceive for years now and you know that I'm drowning in self-pity and embarrassment. I wish I had what you do. But all I have left is hope. Hope that I will too give birth to another generation; hope that we will be rescued from these precarious circumstances."

Mother rose out of her chair just then. "Hope? What good is hope? Our lives and those of our children are at stake. There must be something that we can do! If not for us then for our children!"

"There is…"

"What then?"

"When the time is right, the answer will reveal itself."
"Oh please!"

"Sister, you must have faith."

"Faith?"

"Shhh! Who's there? Khalif?

My mother heard me creeping down the stairs while listening to their conversation.

"Khalif," said my mother, "Are you there?"

"Yes, mum."

"I thought you were writing in your journal."

"I couldn't concentrate."

"What's wrong? You're wheezing!"

I nodded. I took in a huge breath of air, then exhaled.

"Come here. Let me give you a hug."

All I could feel was her warmth, her round figure wrapping around me like a duvet. She was good at that. She could hug away all of the tension, the impatience and the fear.

I stood there and absorbed her warmth until I let out a gust of air.

"Oh Khalif, you're, you're shaking. My son, tell me... what's wrong?"

She pushed me away from her with eyes that penetrated mine. All I could do was return her blank stare.

"Where's your inhaler?"

"It's upstairs."

She got on her knees in front of me and spoke quietly but her hands were shaking as they gripped my shoulders.

"When you feel like this you must get your inhaler straight away. Don't wait. It's better to be safe, my son. It's always better to be safe."

I nodded while she got to her feet. "Now, wait here while I go and get it."

For the rest of the evening I sat by my mother's side while she and my father's second wife, Amala, carried on their usual discussions of social change, political struggle and the shape of things to come. The light inside the house shifted the shadows around the room until the lamp had to be switched on and I began to yawn with heavy eyelids.

Then the door slammed and what followed was a familiar heaviness on the tiles that grew louder with every step. My mother looked over at her co-wife who returned a worried glance before walking over to the mirror to check her reflection. It was too late. He was already in the room.

I saw her posture shift from doting mother to something else, something that made my lips feel dry and the air catch in my solar plexus again.

"Hello, Amir. Why so late, again?"

"Hello, Amala." My father turned to his second wife, his eyes looked heavy and his posture resigned. I had no idea why. All I remember noticing at the time was a fleet of birds floating overhead in a V shape: it seemed ominous in appearance and timing, like a symbol of a future that I could not possibly have known. They passed the moon and for a moment I forgot about the knot in my chest and the cold shivers running down my neck.

"Please,Amala," he said. "leave us!"

*   *   *

The school of fish, oblivious of me as I sink to the seabed, float on above me. They move so gracefully. Is this really what drowning is like? Or is this what it means to die? To accept the hopeless emptiness of life itself and to fully embrace its meaninglessness. No need to breathe or move or fight. Being aware, being conscious. That's all that really matters in the end, isn't it? Being a witness, the witness. Everything starts to go black for a while, so I guess this is it - the darkness that comes for us all when our time is up. A mild astonishment floats to the surface of my awareness. It's a gentle thrill at what this means. Will the answers to the universe finally be answered? But suddenly the blackness starts to weaken, to lighten just a little and after a while I look up to meet my maker and what do I see?

*   *   *

"Khalif, you can't just sit there and pretend that you don't care. Come on, let's go!"

"Larissa you have way too much energy for someone who has just finished all of her exams..."
"That's just it, Khalif. I feel alive again."

"...and too passionate!"

"Like I've been given a second chance to breathe again."

"With a penchant for hyperbole."

She rolled her eyes at me in her usual mischievous way. The gentle current of the breeze made her abaya cling to her figure revealing secrets that I was normally too shy to pry into. I remember her as she was then, round-eyed, boisterous and cunning.

She was the girl chosen by my parents. She helped us by assisting with my mother after the explosion. My poor mother had suffered an attack at the hands of the national army. They had sent rockets into a crowded area where she happened to be shopping for some vegetables. I wasn't there but I heard the blast from school and the desk where I sat writing vibrated.

It wasn't until I got home that I realised something was wrong. Amala was crying. She wouldn't stop hugging me and telling me that it was all right, that everything would be ok.

"Why are you saying this, aunty? What's wrong?"

It took her ages to finally look at me. She held my cheeks in her hands and smoothed the skin of my face with her thumbs.

"It's your mother," she said. "She's in hospital."

"What?"

"Your father's there with her now. There's nothing we can do but wait."

But I couldn't wait. I demanded that I be taken to see her.

The moment I saw her I felt my breath catch in my chest. It felt as though water was building up inside me and that I would drown right there by my mother's bedside. My eyes ran over the bandages that had permeations of redness. My father sat beside her with both of his hands cupping one of hers. He was praying for her, and when he kept looking towards her feet his face would collapse into fits of fury and tearful helplessness. It wasn't until I followed his eyes and looked past her waist that I saw that both of her legs were missing. That's when I drowned in an abyss of unconsciousness.

From that time on, life felt like a dream. Nothing seemed real anymore. My mother didn't really recover, not fully. Every day after that she seemed to be saying goodbye. She wouldn't be able to cook or help with the cleaning, so she would just watch Amala in a helpless daze. I would ask her for assistance with my homework but she would never fully engage.

The time came when mum refused to be transferred to her wheelchair. That's when Larissa started to come by to help. Mum and Larissa bonded immediately. Everyone could see that there was a connection between them. They were kindred spirits. But as every day went by my mother began to talk less and less until the day when she would never speak again.

On that day I was by her side and she was holding my hand. Larissa was there too and she looked at me with an urgency that could only mean that this was the end. But then mum opened her eyes and looked at us both. She took our hands and brought them together till they were in unison. Then she relaxed, her eyes slowly closing and it wasn't long after that that her chest stopped moving.

I looked from her face to my hand that was still holding onto Larissa's. I looked up to find her staring at me, a tear rolling down her cheek. I don't actually remember letting go of Larissa's hands.

*　　*　　*

Emptiness, Silence, Beauty beyond description. Dancing plants of the sea. Fish that play kiss-chase. Water that distorts reality like heat does on a hot summer's day.

*　　*　　*

"Come with me to the top of the hill," said Larissa grabbing my notebook, "or you'll never see this again."

I sprang up from my seat before I knew what I was doing. The fatigue that was making me feel leaden had suddenly disappeared. She had my book in her hand and she was holding it above her head. She wasn't running away but walked backwards to a cupboard till there was nowhere left to go. She rested herself on the edge of it and I eyed the book, my book, my journal, my life history that she held in her hands.

"Give it to me." I demanded. "Give it back."

"Say please."
"Larissa! I'm asking kindly."

"I know and so am I. I just want to do something daring for once. Please, let's go to the hill."

I moved closer as if to intimidate her but she didn't move. I reached out for the notebook but she still held it away from me. She smelt of cinnamon and apples. As I reached for my possession I grew more intoxicated by her perfume. Her smiling lips, inches away from mine.

"So what do you say? Shall we do it?"

My mind went completely blank and I'd forgotten what she was talking about. "What?"

"Shall we go?"

Her eyes were inviting, challenging and persistent. We rode the moped to the summit of the hill. I could feel her grinning at me behind my back but I couldn't feel the same kind of thrill that she was feeling. A lot had changed by then. She got off of the bike first and ran the rest of the way up to the top.

"Larissa," I called. "What are you doing? This isn't funny."
"Khalif," she said. "What day is it today?"

I looked at her with wonder, having no idea of what she was referring to.

"Please, Larissa, I need to get back home. My father will be wondering where I am."

"No he won't because I told him we would be spending the evening together."

"What!? Why?"

"You really don't remember, do you?"

I shook my head at what must have been the most obvious thing in the world.

"Well," she said walking towards me. "It's been 365 days since we first came here."

"Oh..." I remembered that day. The sunset was blood red and huge as it crashed into the horizon and bled into the mountains. Those were the days when everything looked shiny and new. When every experience seemed fresh and crisp. When the future seemed like a mysterious present that dared you to open it. Before hope had flown away from me. Before my mother died and left a hole in our family that was impossible to fill.

"I wanted to come here to see if we could live that glorious day again. Do you remember how spectacular that sunset was? And how we could see your house afar in the distance by the shape of the roof and the way it would sparkle as it reflected the rays of the setting sun?"

I nodded. But my mind was full of my mother's memories. We put the moped onto its stand and walked over to that same spot that we stood at one year ago. I tried to see if I could still identify my house out in the distance. It was there but not as brilliant as it was before.

"Do you remember how clear the sky was that day, Khalif? How beautiful the colours were?

I nodded again.

"Remember how dry the heat was?"

"I remember, I remember..." I said, my voice trembling. I took out my inhaler and took two pulls although I think she knew it was to mask my lack of emotional control. She paused and took a step back from me. The moment was a little longer than it had to be.

"Khalif, I've been thinking. I have been thinking about going away to study at a university outside of Aleppo and I want you to come with me."

"What? How? But..."
"You don't have to make up your mind straight away."
"But Larissa, I can't just leave..."
"I've spoken to your father, Khalif."
"What? When?"

"He thinks it could be really good for you to get away and start afresh."
"That's not possible! I can't leave him. He'll be alone."

"He has Amala! He'll be fine." She pointed to our house in the distance. "They are at home now aren't they, together?"

I nodded, "He's all I've got."

She froze then and shifted her weight back as though stunned.

"You know what I mean..."
"Khalif, I know how hard it is." My head shook uncontrollably at those words.

"You know I lost my dad eight years ago. I know it's hard." Each word caught in my throat as I spoke them. "You, can't, understand!"
"I do. I know what it's like to hope that you could go back and change the past. But, Khalif, I realised a long time ago that no matter how much I want

to relive the past, the sun never sets in the same way twice. Once the past is gone it's gone and no matter how much I wish I could see him again, all that happens is I am met with more grief. Sometimes though, I think it pleases him to see me living life to the fullest. That the only way I can feel close to him is by making him feel proud. That's why I want to go and study abroad in England."

"But it's so far!"

She went quiet for what felt like an ocean of time. Her big brown eyes shone like jewels before she closed them and turned away from me. I couldn't understand why this was happening and all so fast. There was no chance to prepare for this, or to know how to respond. So I did the only thing I thought I could at that point which was to find any way of blaming her. To take her positive and forthright nature and make her wrong.

"You brought me all this way just to tell me that you're leaving? How can you?" I watched her shoulders shake and her head bow. Her slender shoulders hunching over.
"No, Khalif. That's not what I came here to ask you." I noticed that the setting sun wasn't the glorious ball of red fire that it was a year ago but instead it was a faint and yellow bulb that hung in the sky.

"I want you to come with me."

"How? There's no way."
"I knew you would say that but..."
"You are great at maths, Khalif. You could easily get a scholarship which would allow you to go to Oxford." She was right. Hassan was already there. He was due to graduate next year from reading chemistry at Cambridge.
"That's not the point, Larissa. My father! I, I can't just leave him."

"Khalif! He'll be fine," She said pointing in the direction of the house once more. "There's nothing to worry about. He's not alone."

Just then, a shadow passed over our heads bathing us in a shadows of confusion and shock. It was one of those grey fighter jets. It flew overhead with the ominous groan of an angry Titan, flying in the exact direction of where Larissa was pointing. I turned to Larissa in abject terror and in her eyes I could see my reflection. We snapped back to attend to the sound of something shrill that came from the plane. Two fireballs were expelled from the vessel. The spectacle was followed by two violent consecutive explosions and within seconds there were giant clouds of dust that reached out as plumes of smoke completely covered the sunset.

*   *   *

I look up to see giant wings. Its presence seems menacing. Is it a ray or a plane? Are those fish or birds that I see in the distance? Down here, where there is no one else to witness, I see a bright shining light that seems to enter the water like a shooting star, landing at the bottom of the seabed. It has a wondrous glow about it, a collage of colours that blend and separate, move and shift around what must be an angelic figure.

*   *   *

"Khalif! Khalif! Come on, we've got to go. Now!" Figures whirled around me like ghosts. I couldn't help but stare into space as the world I had been living in, which was already a disappointment, had been blown away by balls of flame. Everyone seemed to know where they were going and what they were going to do. They seemed to know how they were going to deal with all of this mayhem. Babies and toddlers were yanked off the floor and carried away in a tense embrace. The elderly were being carried in arms, in a fireman's lift or on piggy back. Everyone looked like they had a destination and a plan for where they had to go. Everyone but me. We were standing in front of what was my road. There was nothing left but rubble and all I wanted to do was look for the remains of my loved ones.

"Hey you! Get your head down!" came a voice from afar just before we heard gunshots. The army was moving through our town and mowing people down with their bullets. Larissa pulled me to safety and I heard a bullet ricochet off a wall near to my head. We hid until the army moved through and when we thought it was safe we jumped onto the moped and rode as far as we could. We rode to the edge of the world.

"Look!" said Larissa. "Over there!"

I watched where she was pointing and saw that a boat was afloat on the water beneath us.

"Let's head for that boat!"

"We can't," I said. "It's too far away and we are too high up. That's crazy."

"It's our only hope. We can dive into the water and swim to the ship. They will save us."

"You're mad, Larissa," I said, but she had just got off the moped and left me sitting on it. She stood by the cliff edge which must have been about 25 metres from the water's surface and she started shaking her hands and making as if to sprint.

"Come on! We have to!"

I thought about my mother's grave that would be left unattended in my absence. I thought about my father and Amala trapped underneath all of that rubble. I thought about the uncertainty of whether they were alive or dead. Then I thought about the life that I was leaving behind that had been turned into a war zone. When I realised what I was doing I was already standing next to Larissa, peering down onto the boat that was fast filling up with people.

"Come on!" repeated Larissa. "It's our only option." she said watching the boat.

"But how can you say that?" I shouted. "You can't just expect us to jump! What if…" But it was too late. She was running towards the cliff edge and before I could stop her she was flying through the air. Before I knew what I was doing I could feel the cool sea air on my cheek and the whistle of the wind in my ears, and then I was flying too. It was beautiful, liberating, peaceful.

*　　*　　*

Down here in this underwater world, I can't keep my eyes from squinting from the brilliance as this vision that treads water effortlessly in front of me. He, she or it is beautiful, with hair that moves about and around with a mind of its own. It reaches out to me but all I can do is watch. A light crease forms in the corner of my mouth at the wonder, the splendour of this vision. It's all I can muster. There is no more strength in me for anything else. It continues to lunge for me, this benevolent apparition. Is this the answer, the end? Is this what happens when we draw our last breath? Angels come and rescue us from the darkness of dreams as yet unknown?

It grabs me by the collar and drags me towards the light. I see it in front of me reaching outwards towards the pure brightness which compels us both and beckons us onward.

There is an all-engulfing sound and sensation when I crash into the brightness. I am bathed in its glory, its beauty. Is this what arriving on the other shore of life is like?

"Here, here he is! Take him!" There is a muffle of sound like a group of people talking far, far away.

"Is he…"

"I don't know."

"Come on! Grab him and get him in here."

"Everyone, please help…"

The voices disappear gradually as numbness takes over from my awareness. This awareness that feels like a television screen slowly turning to black.

"Get him up here. That's it."

"Please, Allah, please don't let him…"

"Make room."
"Roll him on his back."

"That's it."

"I hope this works."

"Khalif!? Khalif? Come on. It will be ok."

Their voices, distant whisperings, faint utterances of care and support. A weight bears down onto my chest. It's unbearable. It hits me repeatedly until I feel an overwhelming implosion.

"Ah… at last! That's it!"

And without knowing it, I am lying on my side, feeling pain in my lungs, my stomach, my heart. Water gushes out of my mouth.

"Allah is merciful!"

"God is great!"

My body pants and struggles to control my breath. It does this all by itself. Fighting to regain control. Someone is holding me. My head is on someone's lap as he or she is seated Japanese style. She cradles my chin in one of her hands and stroking my cheek with the other. I look up and see my upside down angel's face. She tilts her head and I can see her properly now.

"My Khalif. We made it."

My breathing is still erratic, the only utterances coming from my mouth are unintelligible murmurs. But any words that I could possibly have then would have betrayed my feelings that are simply beyond description.

"It's ok, Khalif. We are safe now! Do you hear me?" she says caressing the side of my face. "We're on the boat. They're taking us to Europe. We're saved."

My eyes close while her voice ushers me into another world, the next phase of life which will either be our becoming or our undoing. In this new world, will we sink or swim?

Clara olde Heuvel

Being brought up by a German mother, Dutch father and French grandmother has meant that I have always been intrigued by different cultures and languages.

Having a sincere interest in people and the problems they routinely face, whilst dealing with the government or other institutions, motivated me to read criminal law at Utrecht University and graduate *cum laude.*

During my studies I researched whether the non-refoulement principle[i] was breached when southern European states were sending asylum seekers, clearly in need and navigating treacherous stretches of international water, back to North African states, such as Libya.

In 2014 I spent a year working for the Dutch Immigration Office, during which time I interviewed many people seeking asylum.

From 2017 onwards I witnessed the other perspective first hand, as I appealed for asylum seekers at administrative courts when their applications were being rejected by the Immigration Office. During this time, I became more aware of the judicial, social and emotional problems they were facing. As legal counsel I always sought to advise refugees to the best of my ability.

With this story I hope to give readers a sense of the legal obstacles refugees face whilst trying to build a new life in Europe.

A Treasure

(Photo Credit: Matt Cannon unsplash.com)

They were all seated in the back of the van. One woman with a child was sitting next to him. He remembered from stories of friends who had already taken the 'Touareg' route that it could be immensely dangerous. The van could be spotted by soldiers and the drivers could be turned over to the police or even get shot. The road felt stony. This ride cost him about 5000 dollars. He hoped it would be worth it, since he had borrowed the money from his cousin. He tried to close his eyes and doze off for a little while, but the heat in the van and his thoughts wouldn't let him relax.

"Next stop is Tripoli," one of the guys next to the driver shouted. The loudness of that voice woke him up immediately. What time was it? It felt as if he'd only just gone to sleep.

"Ieeeeeeeeet". The van stopped. They almost hit the plate that divided the driver from the passengers. "Thanks for the ride, bro," Obabu said, jumping off from the back.

"You're welcome, bro." The van drove on.

Now he had to look for a place to live. He didn't know where to go; he was new here. He also had to look for a job to save for his upcoming journey to Italy. He knew that was going to cost another 3000 dollars.

Tripoli was huge. It was a port city. Very industrial; he could smell the smog. He was wandering through the market constantly looking around. It was midday. The sun was at its strongest. He felt the sun burning his face, the sweat drops rolling down his cheeks. This was too hot for him. He had to look for some shade.

He saw a tailor's shop on his left, a grocery shop on his right. Next to that was a butcher. Meat was hanging on hooks, in the full heat of the morning sun, covered in flies. It looked disgusting.
He went into the grocery shop and bought some mango with his last cents. His stomach hurt from the hunger, his mouth felt dry.

While walking out of the store he heard brisk footsteps vehemently behind him. Suddenly he felt a hand touching his left shoulder. He turned around and saw a tall man with a beard and a keffiyeh looking at him.

"Young man, where are you from? I could use some help in my shop", the man said.

"What do you mean?"

"I need someone to help me in my grocery shop during daytime," the man replied. This might be a good opportunity, Obabu thought. "What are the hours and wage?"

"It will be from 4am till 7pm, I will pay you 15 dollars a day, if you do your best," the man smiled.

"Be here tomorrow morning at 3.45am, so that I can explain your tasks to you before you start. What's your name anyway?"

"Obabu."

He felt fortunate to have found a decent job in a grocery while he had heard others were sold on the slave market in Libya by daylight.

Through this boss he got introduced to a wealthy family. They needed a cleaner and a cook. He could live in their house, while working for them.

Obabu didn't think he was respected by Arabic people; they looked down on him, because of his colour. He had been beaten up a few times. He was being shouted at and degraded in front of others. One incident which he remembers well....

"You there! You aren't working that hard. You can do much more for me."

"I am feeling so tired though, boss," Obabu replied.

"Are you declining what I say? You will not disgrace me in front of other personnel. Otherwise, you will feel it. Wasn't last time a lesson for you?"

He still felt the scars on his back from that time.

Days past. Months past. His saving money increased little by little.

He was working day and night. No restful moment.
He could only think about his next move and getting out of this place, a place that was so draining.
One day, he still remembers it happened on a Thursday in springtime, a guy, later known to be called Jalala, came up to Obabu while he was working.

"Hey bro! I see you almost every day here. Why are you working so often in this shop?" the guy asked.

"I am saving up money."

"Don't you want to leave to a better place, Europe for example? This work is too hard for you."
"That's my plan. But I still need some more money. I've heard people get charged 4000 dollars when they want to cross. It still lies too far ahead of me."

"Well, you know man…. I know some people who can offer you a good price for the crossing," the guy said in an incentivizing way.

"What would the price be?"

His boss lifted his head, looking very astonished, while he was talking to Jalala. "Hey, Obabu what the hell you think you're doing? You are at work! This is no time to chit chat with customers."

Jalala looked at the vegetables and tried to avoid the attention of Obabu's boss. He started whispering: "Psst, I'm gonna ask my friends over the next few days, will let you know…"

Obabu nodded invisibly.

One girl, who was working in the shop as well, registered the conversation between them. This girl should have been around the same age as him. He sometimes caught her staring at him from behind the fruit-shelves. She didn't look bad. To be frank, she looked quite pretty. Her facial curves were soft, and her lips were smooth. Her skin was light brown. Her eyes sparkled when she smiled. She had dark – hazelnut brown eyes. Though the contact between her and him was quite formal and business-like, he sometimes thought about inviting her for a walk down the medina. From there they could have a romantic view over the port and seaside and have a chat, maybe hold hands for a while and look into each other's eyes and just stare at each other.

"Uhhh, could you please hand me the other aubergine from the back, Mr.Obabu? The basket is empty again."

He immediately looked up and got back into reality when he heard this voice behind him. He saw the girl, who he just daydreamed about, standing behind him, while he was counting the cash.

His thoughts were dwelling off again. He should concentrate on his job!

On the other side he couldn't be blamed for it. He didn't have any social interactions with women since he left Nigeria...

It must have been a week later, when he was counting the cash desk and just tilted his head. All of a sudden, he saw the guy again waving at him. He looked around to see whether there were any clients. "Hey man" Jalala yelled.

Obabu replied: "One sec, brother." He finished counting and put the cash desk quickly away. Then he started walking in Jalala's direction.

Jalala started: "You know man; I talked to my fellas yesterday and asked them what they would charge for the trip. I also told them that you're my

119

friend and a good fella and they shouldn't charge you the highest price. So, it will be around 2000 dollars."

"Hmm, let me see."
"The price is fair man. It's like 50% less than normal you see," Jalala said convincingly. "What kind of boat is it?" Obabu asked.
"It will be a small rubber boat, just for 8 people," Jalala replied.

"Oh no man, we will all drown," Obabu said.
"No way!! The sailors are experienced. They have helped thousands of people cross to Italy. See it from this point; you will be in Europe and have much better circumstances. You know, I met a lot of people who would pay an even a higher amount to get there. I don't know what happened to you in your home country. But you deserve a better life, I am sure about that!"

Obabu saw this as an invitation to start sharing with Jalala what happened to him in his home country:

"You know, I was living in the upper part of Nigeria. I am Christian; my whole family is. But, our religion was not tolerated in that area. We were the only Christians in our village, the rest were Muslims. They are the majority in the north, where I grew up. I wasn't free! I couldn't go to church. I couldn't practise my religion. I was so limited in my freedom and expression. I belonged to a church community and I tried to go to mass every Sunday. But that day of the week was one of the hardest. Often, random guys would follow me and threaten me on the way to mass. They would throw stones at me and insult me. A few times I was beaten up. The church itself almost got burned down. They tried to set it on fire."

"Also, whilst being in secondary school I became friends with a girl 'Imane'. I really enjoyed my time with her. Every Wednesday we would go to the market together. It was a long walk. We would talk for hours on the way there and back. We told each other about our family background; how many brothers and sisters we had, what we didn't like about our parents, what colour we preferred, what food we loved, and which subjects we were interested in at school. We laughed a lot. I asked her what she would want to do in the future. She wanted to study medicine. Her father would not allow it, because she was meant to be a housewife according to his dogmatic view on life."

"And, because I was Christian and she Muslim the contact we had gave her a lot of problems with her whole family, but especially with her father. In the beginning when we met at primary school, we were still young and her family accepted me as a good classmate. Later on, our contact became closer as we grew older. Her family started disallowing her to go with me to the market. Her father dominated the whole family. He was such a strict man; his way was the only way and he couldn't imagine his daughter having a relationship with a Christian. So, I wasn't allowed to see her anymore. Her father just wouldn't tolerate her being seen by the community with me. Sometimes we saw each other secretively. But that came out since neighbours started gossiping. In the end he forbade her to go out at all. She wasn't even allowed to school. She was under house arrest. Her father saw me as his enemy and he threatened to kill me if I came near his daughter, his house and his street again."

"How awful! I feel so sorry for you man. I can't imagine how this must have felt for you. It sounds cruel. I find it very courageous and open that you share this story so freely with me," Jalala said.

"Well, I feel that I can trust you and you seem sincerely interested in me," Obabu replied. "Now, I am even more convinced about you taking this boat!" Jalala shouted out loud. "You honestly deserve it, my friend. Try to arrange the money as soon as possible. And let me know about it. I will return in three days…"

"What days of the week is the boat normally departing?" Obabu asked.

"It depends on my fellas. They will organize all of it, the people, the fuel, the time, everything," Jalala replied. "Don't take too much time, though."

"OK," Obabu answered guiltily.

Obabu was too tenacious to give up. It didn't matter to him in which country he would arrive. His goal was: A better life in Europe.

Jalala kept his promise. He came back exactly three days after their conversation. "Hey! Have you made up your mind now?" he shouted. Obabu was busy sorting all the vegetables and writing it down on a list.

"Yeah, I want to take your offer," he replied very confidently. "What's the plan now? Who should I give the money to?"

"To me, I will forward it to the people who are in charge."

Obabu checked whether there were any customers around. Obabu ran to his bag behind the counter in the other room, in order to avoid conflict with his boss. He got the cash and walked over to Jalala: "When will I hear about the time and meeting point?"

"I will tell you tomorrow morning," Jalala replied and went on: "Be aware, that there may only be a few days in between."

"Good. See you tomorrow," they waved at each other.
From his left shoulder he could see his boss watching him secretively.
After Jalala had gone, his boss came up to him. "What were you thinking? Who is this man that comes and visits you almost every day? What does he want from you?"

"He is my friend," Obabu replied very self-assured.

"What did you just give him?" his boss snapped.

"Nothing, Sir", Obabu replied.

"Hopefully none of my vegetables!" he yelled. His boss had lost his temper again. After cleaning the shop and giving the papers back to his boss, Obabu returned to the house of the wealthy family for which he cleaned and cooked and where he slept.

"Could I speak to you for a minute Mr. Muhamad? I have something on my mind."

"Sure, sit down, what's going on?"

"Well, as you may know, I am looking for options to leave for Europe." Obabu's heartbeat went up.

"Most of you people do," Mr. Muhamad replied very stoic. "So, what are you saying exactly?"

"Well, I met aguyin the vegetable shop. His friends are in charge of the boats that are crossing to Europe. He asked me whether I wanted to have a better life. I talked to him and he offered me a discount," Obabu said.

"And when do you leave?"
'Hmm, well it can be in the coming days or the coming week it depends on those people."

Mr. Muhamad was silent for a minute...then he said: "Hmm. That's a short notice. Of course, I can see your point of view. If that's it, go on with the rest of your work now."

He went on with his work in the shop and at the house as normal.

A few weeks had passed and he didn't hear anything from Jalala until now. He got a bit nervous and insecure. Especially, since Jalala said he would come back the next day. "What if Jalala is trying to rip me off? Maybe he just pretended to be nice and was in fact after my money? Oh my god. I gave him all my money...."

He tried to not think about it and move on, how he had always done in life until now. But still these negative thoughts crept up on him.

123

Then one Friday afternoon, a few minutes before closing times, while Obabu was locking the door of the shop from outside, he saw a young man running towards him from a distance. It was Jalala, for god sake!"Hey! I got you the times and date where you need to be," Jalala shouted excited. "It will be next Friday at 2 pm. You need to be there at 1pm and you leave at 2.30 pm. It will be a rubber boat. The guy you have to look out for is very tall and slim. He has a somewhat longer beard and he always wears a keffiyeh, like your boss in the shop does, you know? His name is Muhammad Abar. Call him Abar."

"What else do I need to know or tell them?"
"Nothing. They are well informed."

He started running towards his house. Obabu was intensely happy.

He fell asleep immediately and slept like a rock. Next Thursday at work, he felt distracted all the time. He weighed the customer's fruit, stacked shelves and checked the incoming orders. All for the last time. He looked at the girl who he had worked with for 3 years now - for the last time…

He could not sleep the night before his departure. He was overexcited, his nerves almost busted. He wanted to get to the harbour on time, so that he could check where exactly he had to be.

He woke up, dressed himself very rapidly and walked towards the port side. He remembered what Jalala told him. He had described Abar perfectly. Abar and the other boatmen told him that they were waiting for a few more people; eight in total. Obabu still had to wait for another 30 minutes. A man counted that they were all there then said out loud "Guys, we are taking you now to a rubber boat that is arriving in a few minutes along this side. You are going together with my colleague Abu the boatman. He will take you to the shore of Italy,"

"Won't the boat sink?" Obabu shouted.

Abu replied: "You never know. We have 160 nautical miles ahead of us, anything can happen," Abu said.

Obabu didn't have time to overthink the situation. It's now or never, he said to himself. If you never take a risk, you never know if something turns out good or bad, because you didn't give it a try. What wisdom, he thought. It was only a few minutes before they departed.

"Guys, let's walk to the shore. Our boat is arriving. On board! As soon as possible, before the coast guards see us and imprison us!" one of them shouted.

They all got on board and the boatman turned on the engine. Their trip had begun.

In the boat he was among nine other people. He sat across from a lady who was holding a young child in her arm. She looked pregnant. Next to her sat some younger kids and an older man, who seemed to be her husband. He looked out on the blue water. It was a bit stormy. The boat went heavily. A few hours later it was totally still on the ocean. Though he constantly heard some shouting and crying, he felt confident. He trusted the boatmen. He took the dark blue water in and drifted off....

"Aaaaa!!" a woman screamed sharply. This cry woke him up immediately. She must have had a nightmare, as it still seemed as if she was asleep.

He tried to sleep some more but couldn't. It was night, but still he could see some flashes of the waves. They were louder than during the day. And the wind had also gotten harder and colder.

After a few hours he saw the sky turning a light orange colour. It was sunrise. He also saw the shore coming closer, and many more boats all wanting to land on the shore of the island they just reached. He later came to be aware this was Lampedusa, belonging to Italy.

Everything was so loud on the coast side. All people arriving on the coast looked exhausted.

They were taken to the shore by people wearing shirts from 'Frontex'. Later he got to know they were the European Border Agency. All people went through gates and their bags were checked. Some had a passport, mainly Syrians. Others didn't have one, or they just threw them away. He knew from the beginning that with a passport you have no chance at all in Europe, since you will be sent directly back to your home country. The Italian authorities tried to take fingerprints of all incoming people but were obviously overwhelmed.

Obabu remembered this procedure very well. After his fingerprints were taken a photo was taken and he was brought by bus to an asylum seeker building. All asylum seekers who entered Italy by sea and wanted to claim asylum were sent to that house. Those people, whose fingerprints were not immediately taken, slipped through the gates to where human traffickers were waiting for them, taking advantage of them.

After a week, Obabu was interviewed by an immigration employee. It was a very short interview. He got a paper on which he had to write down in his own language which countries he had travelled through, what he had paid per travel and to whom, whether he knew the names of the people who brought him to Libya and after that by boat to Italy. He had to write down his means of travel and which cities he had passed through. This was then translated into Italian. After he had written this down, he had to wait in a big room filled with people who all wanted to claim asylum. He had to wait until his name was called. The immigration person told him there was no time limit. He might have to wait a whole day or only for 30 minutes.

Obabu was medically tested by a doctor, otherwise he couldn't legally be interviewed.

When he heard his name shouted out loud he looked up and saw an immigration employee and translator coming toward him. They introduced themselves and the three of them went into a small room. At the beginning of the interview personal information was asked: Where he was born, the name of his parents and grandparents, their jobs, whether they were still alive, who else of his family were still alive in Nigeria, where he went to school, what occupation he had, what he had studied, where else he lived, whether he could name cities close to the town where he lived in Nigeria. The second part was about how he left Nigeria: from which bus station he departed, at what town he crossed the border, which countries he passed through and how he got the money for this journey. They also asked why he lived such a long time in Libya, where he stayed, what he did and what he earned. Also, they asked why he didn't stay in Libya.

The questions were very thorough and direct and after having answered one question, the other question followed straight away.

He then was left in the asylum seeker building where he saw his fellow refugees. The second and last interview by the immigration office would be a week after the first.

Obabu played some soccer with the other refugees at the camp. He got to know one guy from Syria, one from Mali, another from Egypt. They tried to speak English all together and laughed while playing. After the game they sat down to smoke a cigarette and chit chat a bit, talk about crossing the Mediterranean, how they felt about being in the camp and being in Europe. They compared their interviews at the immigration office and how the people that were working at the immigration office were treating them. They talked about whether they were treated friendly and humanely, though never about why they fled their country.

The days passed quickly and the day of the second interview came closer. A different interviewer and a different translator came to pick him up while he was waiting at the refugee building. He was asked the reason for leaving his country. He told them his story.

The interviewer asked very thorough questions, as if she was trying to find a loophole. She asked question after question. She didn't stop. Why did you do this? Why didn't you do that? What do you mean? With whom were you? Where were you when this happened? Which officers from the government did you have problems with? What day was it? Do you still remember the month this happened or that happened? Do you remember the season of the year? Was this in the evening or during daytime? Do you have evidence or any papers to proof this happened to you?

Obabu knew this in advance. The credibility standards were high. The story needed to be logical. It should be realistic and not imaginary. That is what one Eritrean guy told him the first day he arrived at the refugee camp. The interviewer was not taking any side. Her facial expression was neutral. Sometimes Obabu cried, then she would ask him whether he would like to take a break or have some water. The total interview took three hours. At the end she asked him if he was agreeing with everything he had declared during the interview and whether he had further questions.

"When will I hear a reply?" Obabu asked.
She responded: "It will take some months, but it can be sooner."

"Where will I live now?" Obabu asked.

"You will be brought to a big house with other refugees close to the mainland."

What the lady said was true. He was taken to a big house. He lived there together with other asylum seekers. He was given food every day. He had his own bed and blanket and slept in a room together with 15 other people. Italy took care of him. He even made some friends.

Two weeks after the interview he was told that he had been given humanitarian status for one year.

The elation he felt on hearing that didn't last long.

Now he was legally recognized as a refugee and he could stay in Italy, but he was not allowed any longer to live in the big asylum seeker house because he was no longer an asylum seeker. He had to be responsible for himself; the State wasn't going to take care of him. The refugees needed to find their own place to sleep and their own jobs. Since Obabu had no place to go to, he started living on the streets.

Every day he was looking for food, begging at bakery stores for left over bread. Some churches would help people in need, but only for a few days and not every person. Obabu was lucky he was Christian, so some days he was allowed to sleep in a church. But the churches didn't have places for longer than a few days. He was sent out on the streets again. He was in a devastating situation. As he didn't have a job, he couldn't earn money and couldn't pay for food or afford housing. Unfortunately, the Italian government wasn't considerate with that.

He couldn't bear this situation any longer and decided to make his way to Germany, assuming he would be living under better conditions there. He had heard from other refugees that Germany had a stable economy and that companies were looking for people and were open towards immigrants.

Illegally he took a train from Cosenza, in the south of Italy, to Basel. From Switzerland he then hitchhiked to Germany. He didn't know where in Germany he wanted to go. The truck dropped him off in Mind, in the Phalia region. He went to the police office and asked where he could be registered as a refugee. They explained the way to the asylum centre in Mind.

In Mind he had to go through almost the exact procedure as in Italy. Immigration took his fingerprints, asked him all the questions that had already been asked in Italy. They also asked him in which other European country he arrived first and whether he got a refugee status in any of the European countries. He wrote down why he couldn't bear living in Italy any longer. This time they didn't ask him why he left Nigeria, since this was the so-called Dublin procedure: the interview was much shorter than in Italy.

From Mind he got appointed to an asylum seekers' house in Phalia. Vrun was the name of the town. The government supported him with everything: food, blankets, beds, German classes and money to live on. This procedure could take as long as the government wanted and needed it to be, as there was a flood of refugees. Therefore, there was no legal time limit for a decision being taken regarding his status. While he was receiving about 300 euros a month from the social office, he should also be available for some work without getting paid. This was in return for the benefits he received.

A few weeks later, Obabu found an internship at a company that specialized in window frames. He was meant to undergo the internship for six months. The job agency agreed to it and the asylum benefits continued alongside the internship.

He showed his best capacities to this company. He was motivated and started learning to speak more German.

The internship went very fast. His boss appreciated all the work he did and that he was such a fast learner. He got offered an employment contract for three months.

Because he got along very well at his workplace, he was – after the three month period – offered a one-year contract.

One day he returned home after work and he saw a brown envelope in his post box. There was a stamp and a date on it. It seemed important. He could feel his heartbeat going up! He was anxious. What could be inside the letter? From whom could it be? The government? The benefits agency? Maybe the immigration office? He couldn't stop guessing. He had been living in Germany for more than two years now. He ripped open the envelope. He had to know what was inside.

Inside was an introduction letter and a second document with more pages stapled to each other. His German language level was not that high yet. He could only understand one sentence in bold letters on the first page of the second document: "not granted". His world turned upside down.

He knocked heavily on the door of Mrs Punak, with the letter in his hand. She was a trustworthy person from Human Resources at his company.

Mrs Punak opened the door and looked at him. "What's wrong?"

"Look! This letter is a negative. Could you please read what it exactly says?", Obabu cried.

Mrs Punak explained to him that the immigration office had taken a negative decision on his asylum request, because he had already been awarded a refugee status in a European country – Italy. He had 30 days to leave Germany and after deportation there would be a ban for five years of re-entering the European Union. If he wouldn't leave voluntarily, he could be deported from Germany to Nigeria or Italy, the first country he arrived at.

"You can appeal the decision. You have one week, Mr Obabu. I will find a law firm for you specialized in asylum and make an appointment with them. OK! Come back to my office in a few hours please."

Some hours passed, and he returned to her office.

"I booked an appointment with a legal advisor at a law firm in Grinwald for tomorrow. Go there in your lunch break."

"You are one of our best employees. You know that, that's why we will try to find a solution for you."
He knew that. He was so blessed with his employer. This company gave him a chance, because he was from a different country and willing to learn something.

The next day at 1.30pm day he would meet Mrs Horst at the bus stop across from his company, a lady who knew Mrs Punak as well.

While he was walking towards the station he saw an elderly lady waving at him in the distance. "How are you Mr. Obabu? My name is Beate Horst," she said. "Could you give me the negative decision from the government so that I am prepared for the meeting with the lawyer? I can read it while sitting on the bus." He handed her the file.

Mrs Horst explained to him that there were five important things written in the decision. He already knew this when Mrs Punak explained the letter to him yesterday. "Oh! Mr Obabu this doesn't sound good at all..."

He had not yet been to Grinwald. What did he have to do there? He worked and lived in Vrun.

The bus driver started shouting the stops on the way, because the technology did not work. "Next stop Grinwald city!" the bus driver yelled.

"We have to get out here, Mr Obabu! Hurry up." He took his bag. "It's not far from here, I googled it. The law firm is located ten meters from the bus stop. Look over there!" Mrs. Horst said.

There was a legal advisor who specialized in asylum law. She welcomed him into the office.

"The letter means that you are in a Dublin procedure and we only have a week to appeal. The weekend was already included in that calculation. I will do all I can, and I start to work for you when you have paid the deposit of 250 €. This appeal costs about 496 € in total but you can pay 50 Euros a month in instalments," Mrs Koenig explained.
Obabu jumped out of his chair and went out of the law firm to withdraw the money immediately.

Three weeks later he was being called again to the law office.
Mrs Koenig started the conversation: "So in the urgent procedure before the Court we got a negative ruling. This means that you can be sent to Italy at any moment."

"How can that be? I already told them everything," Obabu said.

"I know. It's because of the Dublin III Regulation. That says that the first country in which you arrived needs to take you back. Especially when you have received humanitarian status there. It was a political decision by all the member states of the European Union to create this system with the first country of arrival. The second country where you arrive doesn't even look at the reason why you left Nigeria. Since Italy had already given you a humanitarian status. You are already protected in a sense." Mrs Koenig explained.

"But, my humanitarian status has already expired for two years. It's not valid anymore. You know I lived in total poverty in Italy. While I was awaiting my asylum decision I lived in a house with other asylum seekers; the government paid for that. But after I was granted a humanitarian status they just told me to look for my own place. They would only help people who had just arrived and awaited their asylum decision, not the ones who already obtained something. I could not find a job in Italy and therefore I could not have my own apartment. Of course, I was looking for a job but the employment situation in Italy is so bad, even for the Italian nationals. So, in the beginning I had some friends, who I met while I was in my asylum procedure. They let me sleep at their place, but after a while they couldn't afford it anymore to have me over. I slept outside close to a bridge, so I wouldn't get wet when it was raining. It was so cold outside, especially during winter nights," said Obabu.

"I have read about the situation in Italy. There are some churches that help but unfortunately, they can only take a maximum number of people. One positive thing may be that there is a court in Hannover that issued a court decision in which it ruled that sending asylum seekers who have applied in Italy for asylum back to Italy would be a breach of Article 3 of the European Convention of Human Rights. That article proclaims that no person shall be subjected to inhuman or degrading treatment. If a court takes such a stand then that person cannot be sent to the first country of arrival, but the asylum seeker needs to undergo his procedure in the second country, in this case Germany. Some courts said this about Greece for example, since Greece was overwhelmed with asylum seekers. This means that the country does not live up to a human standard for the asylum seekers arriving there. Some courts even found that sending asylum seekers back to Hungary was not in accordance with Article 3. Asylum seekers were tortured there and had to live in cages like animals. But with Italy most courts don't see a breach to the Article 3 rule. The courts are divided."

"Anyway, the court in the emergency procedure might have now ruled negative. Still the German immigration office needs to request from the Italian authorities whether they are willing to take you back and by when. So, we need to wait anyhow."

He went home, devastated.

At work he was called into Mrs Punak's office again.

"Mr Obabu, I will call your law firm and talk to the legal advisor to see whether they can do more for you." She started explaining, while Obabu was listening to the telephone conversation: "You must know Mrs Koenig we really didn't expect that Mr. Obabu would learn so quickly. At this moment he is covering for his supervisor at the sawing machine, because that person is on sick leave. But before he got sick, he taught Mr Obabu everything. Mr Obabu can do the job all by himself now! It's amazing. The colleague will be ill for a longer period and you know what? Mr Obabu will now take his supervisors' responsibilities at the sawing machine and will even teach other colleagues how to saw. He works so independently. We are truly astonished."

"I completely understand your point of view. Unfortunately, the Dublin regulation doesn't leave any room for interpretation or personal issues. There is only one court that took a different opinion on Italy and didn't apply the Dublin III regulation," Mrs Koenig replied.

"Our manager can and will send you a recommendation for Mr Obabu," Mrs Punak said.

"That could be extremely helpful! In parallel to this asylum procedure I could ask for a work permit and through that Mr Obabu might have a right to stay here if the authorities are willing to give him a stay based on work," Mrs Koenig said.

When the letter arrived at the law firm, Mrs Koenig read it with great astonishment. It was purely positive. It stated that Mr. Obabu was irreplaceable. There is just not enough qualified German personnel to choose from. The company explained that they would truly lose a lot of know-how if Mr Obabu would not bearound anymore. Besides, Mr Obabu integrated very well in the team from a personal perspective. Other colleagues told that he was punctual, helpful and trustworthy. They expressed that they would not be willing to lose a good employee and that everything he built so far in this country could be destroyed within a second. They also stated that they did not understand this legal procedure either from an economic or from a human perspective.

She sent it immediately to the council and asked for a working permit.

Six months passed and still he hadn't heard from the lawyer or from Mrs Punak. Obabu hadn't slept well for the last few days. He was thinking back about the situation in Nigeria. He had worked so hard at this company. He got promoted to a higher position. Now he was even teaching other people the work he had done for the last one and a half years. That gave him a satisfying feeling. He had achieved something in his life. They were grateful for having him in the company. They often gave him compliments.

This whole situation to be sent back to Italy had really confused him. He paid taxes in Germany, he paid his rent, he could afford his living. What else do they want from him? If that is not a reason to stay in a country, then what is? He felt devastated. He cried silently.

He thought back about his past relationship, when the father of the girl didn't want him. That situation was comparable to this one. He loved Imane so much and if they had grown up in a different country than Nigeria, where there would have been more freedom, then they could have been together. He knew that from within his heart.

He was fantasizing about what she was doing at the moment. Whether she was missing him too? Whether she was also thinking about him? Whether she was still angry that he had left. Whether she would be studying medicine now? Six years had passed. He felt so sorry he hadn't had a chance to say goodbye. Would he even remember her, if he was to see her again?

"Good day, Obabu speaking. Can I come by today?"

"Yes, but you need to have an appointment. Please give me your name," the lady replied.

"Obabu O-B-A-B-U", he spelled it out loud. "Tiallo, my first name Madam."

"What is your date of birth?"

"01.01.1988."

"Hmm, let me check when I can book you in today." He waited for a few seconds. "3 pm, does that work?"

"Yes. See you then." He put his phone in his pocket.
He needed to speak to a doctor. He felt a bit sick. Sometimes he vomited his food all of a sudden.

"Today I need to go to the doctor around 3pm is that ok? I do not feel well."
"Yes sure." Mrs Punak replied.

Around 2pm he took off from work to go and see his doctor.

"So Mr Obabu .... What is your concern? What can I do for you?"

"I don't feel that well. I sometimes need to go to the bathroom and vomit all my food all of a sudden."
"Hmm, that doesn't sound great. Are you having stress at the moment?"

"Yes, my status is not clear in Germany. They gave me a negative result. I might need to go back to Italy. That is what the court wrote at least. I feel insecure about my future."

"I understand. You sure have a lot of stress at the moment. I advise you to take some time off."

"I want to work though! This work is the only thing in my life that is going well. I don't have anything else in life," Obabu said.

"Yes, but if you go on like this you can have a serious disease. You must take your rest when your body requests it."

"What do I do when I cannot work Doctor? I don't know what to do. I feel so bored at home."

"Do something nice for yourself: relax, sleep, listen to music, look outside the window, find some sport, talk to friends," the doctor replied.

"Hm, maybe you are right," Obabu said.

"I will prescribe you something for your vomiting and something for stress. It's not chemical, it's a vegetable medicine."

"Thank you, doctor."

"You are free to come back anytime, if it doesn't get better. And remember to take some time off and relax."

"I will try."

He went home and bought the pills on his way. He opened the refrigerator immediately and looked what he could prepare himself.

"I didn't have fish in a long time..." he smiled.

He cleaned the salmon and dried it with some paper. Put some lemon and some salt on it. Then he started peeling the potatoes and washed them. He started boiling the water and left them inside.

"Ding!" His cell phone rang. He went to the table in the living room and checked his phone. On the screen, it said +234. "Nigeria?" he thought. "Now, who can that be?" The only person who has my number is my nephew, who lent me all the money.

He opened the message. The message loaded: "Hi brother, how are u doing? u in Germany now. good 4 u. u still remember me? ur nephew, David gave me ur number... u need to know something. I could not tell u this earlier because I only found out a short time ago that u left the country. I thought u were dead. I was asking around. No one in our village saw u."

"Ding!" A second message arrived while he was reading this. He was flabbergasted.

It read: "then I heard that David was ur nephew. So, I went to see him and he explained to me that u requested asylum in Europe. Txt me back, brother. Rgrds Ali."

"Who is this?" He thought. "I do not know anyone called Ali."

He went back in time. All his childhood memories passed by. He wondered out loud. He couldn't come up with the link to the person.

"Pling!" The oven alarm sounded. "Oh no the potatoes!" he totally forgot about those.

He pressed into them with a fork. They were too soft.

He put his salmon into the pan and left it for six minutes in total three minutes per side. Now he would not let himself be distracted again by his phone.

The salmon tasted delicious, but the potatoes were horrible.

He sat on his couch and watched some TV.

Around 10pm he felt so tired. He went to bed. The next day he would have to work again. His alarm would be ringing at 5.45.

He dozed off immediately with Ali on his mind....

He woke up all of a sudden. His blanket was all wet. His body was soaked in sweat. He looked at the alarm: 2.33. "What? It's not even time to wake up yet...pffff." He dozed off again. He had totally forgotten about Ali.

"Tututut" "Tutuuutttt" Oh no", he thought. His body felt exhausted. He turned off the alarm and went straight to the bathroom and hurried to his work.

At work all things went well. He was sawing some new window frames. He was focused on his task. Suddenly it struck him that he knew Ali.

He stopped the saw immediately and sat down. "Ali! I know Ali," he said out loud.

"What, please?" Mark, his colleague said.

"Well, I got a message from a certain Ali. A guy from Nigeria who I am supposed to know. But I couldn't remember. Just now while I was sawing this window frame it struck me!"

"Oh, that's good. Was there something important in the message," the colleague asked.
"I am not sure..." He thought about that for a while.
He knew Ali from his girlfriend Imane. He was her cousin. Ali knew they had a relationship. Ali also was aware about all the troubles he and Imane had with her father. Ali always expressed sorrow for him, that his uncle was being such an idiot and so conservative, not letting his own daughter choose who she loved and what she wanted in life.
He felt so tense. He could feel his heart beat go up while his sweat rolled down his face.

Again, to the toilet. The breakfast he had just eaten came towards his throat again. He reached the toilet right in time and threw up everything.

"What was that?" his colleague asked. "Are you ok?"

"Yes, but I just have some problems with my health. The doctor says it's stress. I sometimes just have to vomit," Obabu said.

"That doesn't sound good." his colleague expressed.

"He gave me some plant pills," Obabu said.

"Aha, hmm I could give you the name of my specialist. Maybe he can tell you more about your health issues. Take care please," his colleague said.

"Let's get on with our work," Obabu said while looking at the frames and started sawing again.

He put his bicycle in the barn. In his living room he grabbed his phone and started typing a message, a response to Ali: "What is going on Ali? I have responded late, but that's bcs I couldn't make the connection at first when you txtd me. How are you? What is going on? Yes, I am in Germany. I live here. I have a job, I pay my own rent, I learned German! My refugee situation is still unclear. I am awaiting my permit."
He pressed 'send'.
He put away his phone and went outside for a walk. Listening to what the doctor had told him. Seeing trees and smelling flowers, took his mind off his stressful situation for a while.

When he returned from the walk he opened the door. Again, a message. He ran to his phone lying on the shelf.

Ali again. He opened it fast. It loaded: "good to hear from u, brother. Oh I am so sorry that ur situation is unclear. I have to tell u something very important. can u call me back. It's night here so maybe u can call just before I go to sleep?"

He dialled the number.

"Hi Ali, so what's up brother? Long time no see. Six years it has been right?"

"So Tiallo, this is very important." Ali said. Ali always called him by his first name. They were close.

"I thought you might want to know this. I couldn't get in contact before. I don't know why. I tried everything. It took me so long. Everyone thought you were dead. I couldn't believe that though. Later on, I got in touch with your cousin," Ali was speaking so rapidly. "What's going on Ali? Is there something I should know?" Obabu asked.

"I am so sorry, Tiallo. To tell you this so late. After six years!! Really you have to trust me. You want to know this. It's about your life. But don't be mad. OK." Ali said.

"I'm listening."

"So …. I was so astonished when my cousin Imane, who you were together with, left a few weeks after you did. She also went to Germany! Did you know that? She was so sad when you left. Before you left of course she wasn't allowed to go outside anymore. Her father forbade it. After you left she was let outside. But she did not want to go outside anymore. She stayed only in her room lying on the bed. That's what I heard from her mother anyhow. She literally locked herself in her room, wasn't speaking to her parents anymore. I think it had an enormous impact on her that you left," Ali explained.

"I know. I felt so sorry. It still hurts me now, that I could not say goodbye. I could not live any longer in Nigeria. You know that. There is no freedom there, not for me being Christian. And besides that, your uncle would never have agreed on us being together. It was a big hardship for me. I couldn't stand it anymore. I was looking for a way out. And no, I didn't know that Imane is in Germany too," Obabu said.

"I understand you Tiallo. But Imane was immensely sad, she told me many months later via Internet, after she fled the country. She could not understand that you left without saying goodbye. She thought she was the love of your life."

141

"I would have, if your uncle wouldn't have threatened to kill me," Obabu said.

"What?" Ali shouted. "He did that?"

"Your uncle told me: Don't come near our house anymore and never get in touch with my daughter again. If you do so I will have you killed. That's what your uncle said, Ali! Didn't you know?" Obabu shouted.

"If Imane would have known this happened, she would have understood everything. It would have made so much more sense to her why you left and why you didn't say anything. Anyway..." Ali continued. "I heard via a close friend of hers that she had a health issue before she left. She also needed to leave the country because of that. If her father would have found out what she had done she would have been killed. She trusted only this friend with this information. I heard this news also very late, brother," Ali said.

"What is it?" Obabu said.

"You really do not know this, brother?"Ali asked.

"No. I don't."
"So Imane didn't tell you that she was pregnant?"

"Bam!" his phone dropped on the floor.

He looked at the white walls. His world stood still. He couldn't think straight anymore. He was in shock.

"What! Is this true? Ali. Oh my God. Why didn't you tell me this earlier? I have a child. What the f*ck! I am a father. I can't believe it," Obabu was overwhelmed.

"You are, Tiallo. I am so happy I could tell you this brother,"

"Do you know where she lives and how I can meet my child, Ali? I am so overwhelmed with this news."

"As I told you Imane is in Germany too. I could maybe find out for you. But beware six years have passed Tiallo. She will have continued her life. Really be aware," Ali said.

Obabu thought about it. Six years is such a long time now. She could have gotten married to a German man possibly and built her new life. Even though, he was so glad to have heard that he is a father. He felt so proud. He would have never thought that.

It didn't take much longer than three days before he got a new message from Ali, it read:

"Hey bro, I found out where your son goes to primary school. The name is Gartenschule in Obrick city."

He knew Obrick. It was about 1.5 hours by train from where he lived. He could just go there one day during the week around 12am when the children would have an afternoon break and find out about his son. He really wanted to know.

The train ride was quite long. He was lucky to have gotten a day off. There was much to do at work. He checked on the internet in advance how he would get to the school.

It was a 20 minute walk. He arrived before the break. He could hear children running out of the doors up onto the playground. Parents were standing there waiting for their kids. He didn't see a glimpse of Imane. Maybe her new husband would be waiting for his son.

He didn't stand close to the schoolyard. Just a bit further away from where he could just observe everything. He didn't want it to look obvious nor suspicious. He was looking at all the children that ran through the doors. They were free for today. He knew from his colleagues that Wednesdays was a day where the kids were off in the afternoon.

Suddenly he saw a light skin coloured young boy about 45 inches tall running to a lady standing more to the left side of the schoolyard.

The boy looked excited, he was wearing a yellow jacket, he had dark curls and a big smile. His face looked like his, when he was a kid. The inner peace, fulfilment and happiness Obabu sensed at that exact moment in all parts of his body radiated instantly from him.

He could shout it out from the rooftop that he had a son and finally had seen him for the first time! Though he couldn't make a scene here at the schoolyard. So, he pulled himself together.

From where he stood he was trying to look if he could see to whom his son ran to. Though the parents were facing him with their backs. He then recognized her long black thick hair. She wasn't wearing a headscarf. He tried to walk a bit more down the road to his left to see if he could get a glimpse of her face.

Only a few second passed, as she was then suddenly turning her head to interact with another parent standing next to her right side, he could see the right part of her face...

Brigitte Fitschen

I am the daughter of a German father and a French mother who met during the Second World War in Moulin sur l'Allier and married in 1942 in Hamburg. I was born in a village in Lower Saxony 50km away from Hamburg and grew up on a farm with my brother Werner. After my A levels I studied in Hamburg. I interrupted my studies to work for one year as an Assistant teacher at two Sixth Form Colleges in Cambridge. In 1979I finished my philological study in Anglo and American literature and in Romance languages. Following two years of teacher training, I became a secondary school teacher of English and French for several years in Hamburg.

At the age of 34 I immigrated to the Netherlands to marry a Dutch man with whom I have three wonderful children. We later divorced and I fell in love with an African man. I attained a degree as a trainer in multicultural communication and social competency. Through study and my experiences with people who had escaped their country because of torture and misery, I gained deeper understanding, knowledge and skills in diversity, integration and immigration issues.

I have an unwavering passion for painting and sculpting. At the age of 18 my desire was to study Art. I failed to do so because of my father's disapproval. Fortunately, my passion and enthusiasm for art never faltered. For more than 30 years I trained myself to be a painter.

In the past year I have taken up another passion and connected to the Writers Empowerment Club in England to make a 20 year old dream come true by becoming a self-published writer.

One Love

Suriname Lady painted by B. Fitschen (artist's name"Gitti")

What a lovely sunny day! Finn awakes with the sharp sound of his alarm. He is not yet fit to find the button to stop it. Sleep troubles his sight. And his body is aching, leaning on his arms to reach the phone. What a dull thought passes his mind. His heart is immediately heavy while God's creation radiates light into his sleeping room. "How can life be so cruel?" Sunlight everywhere, but in his heart and mind there is mainly darkness. Let's start this day with a morning prayer. God is good, he is almighty, and he is going to help him find a way out of this misery he is in.

He came from Abuja by plane to Italy. How? He has forgotten. He does not want to remember his past life anymore. Europe, a new perspective, a new start! God and he made a pact to work it out together. God promised him to create miracles. He had already fulfilled on one miracle by finding his way through the airport gates with the passport of his dead twin brother.

It's Sunday, the church service will start at 2pm. He is going to meet a guy for whom he sells some goods. He works in a club where he helps guests to enjoy themselves with drinks, joints and flirts. Their tips enable him to survive.

He left Africa because his life was in danger. His boyfriend got killed. Sometimes when he was alone he heard Brian's voice talking to him right in his ear going straight to his heart. He never shared this with anybody because people would have seen it as weird. This was their secret, Brian's and his. Beyond death they were still connected and one. They were looking for him, too. He escaped in time before anyone could have harmed him.

Yesterday, there was Vincent, his sugar daddy. Vincent, a crazy Italian guy who he'd met in the club shortly after his arrival in Italy. The telephone rings:

"Hello, it is Astrid. How are you doing?"

"Oh, Astrid, is it you? Nice to hear from you! I am fine and you?"

"I'm ok. Could we meet? Is that possible? Today? Yes, I am free and you?"

148

"Let me see!"

Vincent who is trying to pull himself out of the blankets, mumbles, "Are you going to meet that bitch?"

"It is none of your business," Finn replies while he is holding his hand over the phone.

"I would love to. Does 4pm suit you, honey?"

"Perfect. Let's meet at the fountain."

"Ok. See you!"

Vincent coming from the kitchen, shouts, "You are not going to meet Astrid, are you?" Vincent approaches.

"Do you know what you mean to me? Don't disappoint me, you mean so much to me. Since I came to know you, my life shines. I feel alive through you." Vincent embraces him pushing his fat belly close to him. Finn turns his head away to avoid Vincent's mouth and bad breath. "Look what a day! Come and watch." He pulls himself out of Vincent's arms to go to the window and watches the neighbours' kids playing in the street.

One of the children's voices reminds him of his elder sister Jamila. He felt so close to her. She was like a Mum to him, the good version of a mother, the loving one not the punishing one. Jamila, how long has he not thought about her. He buried the sorrow about her being robbed by terrorists deep in his bones. Otherwise he would have otherwise killed himself and others! The pain is and was unbearable to feel.

His childhood was with Granny in one of those sweet villages. Granny and Grandpa taking care of them while Mum and Dad went to the city to find work.

"Honey, please come. I will give you a good time." Finn could not believe the need and greed for sex this elderly overweight man had. Vincent was insatiable, as if he had never been loved nor had sex before in his life.

"Hey Vincent, I am not your toy, nor a sex machine," Finn replies.

"Darling," Vincent waves a one hundred dollar note in one hand. "Baby, come and give me a good time. You know I will enjoy it!"

"Wow! It's so great. You're so good to me, gosh!"

What does a man have to go through to achieve his humanity? He has to prostitute himself only to survive. He might be obliged to do things he never would have done before to a human being. He truly feels ashamed. How could he become such a deceiver? To kiss and to make love to someone he would not have considered, under different conditions, to become a possible lover. However, Vincent would not give up. He was used to getting what he wanted. Finn was better off doing him this favour in order to have peace afterwards than resisting him. "Do you like this?" Finn asks falsely.

Finn rushes to the shower. Then dries him self and dresses for going out. What a shit affair. He leaves to meet Astrid.

Astrid had nearly finished her PhD. She came to Italy three years ago and had enjoyed her life a lot. Her work as a PhD student was a success and her love life had been successful, too. She would go out to the club alone, but never returned alone. Most of these lovers just got accepted once. A few managed to return over a couple of weeks because they managed to maintain her interest throughout the day, and mainly accompany her through some lonely nights. Astrid had what they call in German 'Klasse'. She was an amazing girl. She was tall, lean and blonde and she loved to talk and to make love. And one never felt bored with Astrid. She laughed and smiled throughout the day as if she was born to be a happy winner in this life.

Although her study was abstract, Astrid acted spontaneously and socially and was very interested in black people coming from abroad, from another world, another continent, Africa. She especially showed interest in men who differed a lot from Europeans. They attracted her interest in the exotic and this was reciprocal. They seemed to be so compatible. The interest in the duality of each other was obvious.

Astrid had been in a relationship with an African man she had fallen in love with at the age of 20. His name was Damian. He shared and taught her a lot about his home country Eritrea. She came to know him in Hamburg, in one of those student residences where she lived during her study. After having been friends for two years they fell in love with each other romantically. He was the first man with whom she experienced the pleasure of an orgasm. Being together for three years with her German boyfriend she did not yet know that pleasure.

Meanwhile Astrid's parents and her boyfriend made her feel their disapproval. It seemed to be a non-spoken agreement that Astrid should not be with a black man, only a white man. And that it was inappropriate to leave a decent white boyfriend with a good future as a CEO for a black student of sociology and politics who did not have any future and could not offer her any security at all. Moreover, coming from an African patriarchal society where men were the bosses, not the women. She did not imagine him to be a possible husband. How could that work out? African men were supposed to be deceivers in a committed and monogamous relationship. Headlines appeared in her head. "Emancipated young talented woman and black political African student looking to settle down in Germany." On the one hand, it was morally wrong; she would have to leave her boyfriend, with whom she was supposed to stay with her whole life. On the other hand, being with Damian was doomed to fail because of the big gap in their socio-cultural backgrounds. Avoiding making her own choice, she ran away to Italy instead.

When Astrid saw Finn for the first time, she thought "what a handsome man, what a beauty he is, looking like a prince." That was the reason she opened her heart and her femininity to him. He inspired her by his interesting political talks, his humour that was always present all the time, and his friendliness towards her and others. He reminded her of Damian, her only happy love which she denied herself because of being a coward to face her life, giving away her power to her parents and her German boyfriend. This time she knew for sure that she wanted to be bold and adventurous, and passionately give herself to life and love. Finn had a lot to say and she never felt lonely or bored with him. Astrid had profundity and at the same time she had the ability to enjoy herself like a child. She was not only a brilliant talker, but also a very compassionate listener. Finn loved this German young woman. She had discipline and straightness, appearing to him a powerful and self-assured lady. And she was very pretty and sporty. He liked a woman who took care of herself.

Bernd who was a doctor, was going to come to take them across the border. Finn was supposed to crawl into the trunk of the car to avoid any problems with the police. Having a black man in one's car causes suspicion. Better not to tempt fate. People are nosy, always imagining the worst scenario of life. One had to be careful.

Italy seemed to be a sweet place to live; many cafes and young dynamic women and men. He understood why Astrid loved to stay here as long as she could permit herself. There was fun to experience, mainly for rich white citizens. However, as a black refugee it was hell. No accommodation, no food, no social system to fall back upon. You just had to cope with life yourself. You were registered and not sent home. You were not killed or expelled, but for the rest of the time you were left alone to find your own way.

In Germany, the country where refugees and asylum seekers are taken care of, refugees are welcomed with clothes, food, a bed, pocket money, and hospitable, kind, social people working as volunteers to help the downtrodden find their way. People adopt or mentor one or two foreigners. They have them stay in their houses and make them feel at home. They help with money because they are good people kindly sharing their income with the poorest and neediest. He loves the German social system. Of course, you have some racists, but the majority are open-minded people, not hiding their emotions. When they like you, they support you. There are lots of pretty women who want to help, ready to walk right into a relationship with a foreign man.

Astrid could help him, he knew that, but he also knew that she was a romantic. She wanted to be loved and to love. She could not help him in this. She was not the woman for that. Again, he had to pretend to be in love! Every heterosexual man would have loved to come to know a lady like Astrid, only he was not hetero. And he hated to lie to people who were his friends. When could he stop with lies, being a deceiver and betrayer? He hated himself! Astrid was charming and sweet, a very understanding woman. Just like his Mum! He respected women and did not want to harm them. Finn had thought it over several times to be open hearted with Astrid and share his sexual preferences. However, it seemed as if something was holding him back. It was his fear, but also his instinct that told him to keep this to himself. He longed to open up to someone with whom he could share the sadness, the pains and sorrow about his sweetheart's death.

When Finn lived in Nigeria he went from Abuja to Ibadan for the marriage of a good friend. He was his best man. What a lovely celebration. With a wonderful bride and bridegroom. His friend was from England whose parents had immigrated 20 years ago. The father was a veterinarian who found work in a Dutch chicken company on the outskirts of Ibadan and was asked to be part of the management. At the wedding celebration, he met lots of different people, some English ones whom had also come over for the wedding celebrations. There he met the love of his life, Brian, a tender young guy, tall and relaxed with a somehow little ironical smile on his face. He was very polite and extremely good looking. Wow! It was love at first sight. Brian's appearance hit him like cosmic energy.

He approached him, and Brian understood his intention at once. They had the same sensuality and sensitivity, the same spirituality. Many words were not necessary to understand each other. They felt connected from the first moment they met each other. Brian made a request from his boss to stay a fortnight longer. Oh, how he missed the time they had spent together! The sweetness of feeling united, deeply in love with each other. Never in his life had he passed so many wonderful days and nights in the company of another human being he was in love with. They were the perfect match. They went to clubs, danced together in bars and spent night after night in his friend's home where they made use of a tiny studio with bathroom and kitchen. They were safe there in that protected residential area of Ibadan. But somehow it spread that Brian was homosexual. He was threatened and blackmailed. Brian didn't give a shit about being threatened. Finn held him back, but Brian was a stubborn Scottish guy who ignored intimidation. He stood for being different. Then, one day when he went to the market alone, Finn was visited by Police who came to tell him that Brian, his beloved friend, had been stabbed by fanatics and that he had died there before the ambulance had taken him to the hospital. Finn froze. He isolated himself and became invisible in front of everybody. No matter how much they begged him, his decision was made to escape from this country as soon as possible. He could not live anymore in a country like his own, where as a citizen one had to hide one's preference, where any vulnerability you showed, could mean your death sentence.

Africa was a hard culture, certainly no place for gay men. One had to be a real man that God wanted, a man as it was written in the Bible. Be fertile and reproduce yourselves as male and female! It was written in the Bible that men had to be the head of a family. A couple had to make children. That it was their duty as a correct, devoted Christian couple. This harshness, the lack of a humanitarian consciousness, this traditional belief in the Bible proved to him that Mother Africa was a hard continent to live in, merciless for those who did not conform to these rules and dogmas of the country. Finn started pitying himself by saying, "Oh my God, why have I lived with fear and violence my whole life? On top of that, I am being pressurized and threatened by death."

Finn remembers his mummy Dora. She was a bold and very kind woman. A mother he had admired and was fond of as long as he could remember. She was stressed by that narcissistic father of his. He hated that man who called himself a father. This was the bossy, proud, and aggressive father Finn had been afraid of his whole life. Mum had to calm him down permanently with all sorts of tricks to keep them safe. She tried hard to protect her babies, her treasures from being mistreated by this grisly man they had to call and refer to as 'Sir'!

"Hi Astrid," Finn hugs her in a gentle way!

"Hi Finn," she replies kissing him vividly on his cheeks! "You look a little tired. Is everything going well with you, Finn? This is Bernd, my dear friend from Hamburg."

"Hello Finn!"

"Hello Bernd! You are this brilliant guy who worked for Doctors Without Borders. Nice to meet you. Astrid has already told me a lot about you. She really admires your 'engagement'. I envy you having such a fulfilled life. You live from a powerful vision. Thank you being here to meet me and offering your support to take me out of Italy. I am very grateful to you!"

Bernd, who lives for his profession and his political and social views, thanks him by offering him a lovely smile, putting his hand on his shoulder. Then he says, "You are welcome, my brother. Are you all right? Let's take a seat here." He orders three Espressos and starts directly with the issue that has brought them together. "Finn, I think we should not lose time. I propose to set out immediately. Are you ready to leave?"

Finn looks at him nodding his head enthusiastically. "I am ready to go! Can't wait any longer, the quicker things go, the better I will feel."

"Okay man, that's a deal. Tomorrow the weather will change. The weather forecast is for heavy showers with lots of rain. I propose to make use of that for our departure. The Customs Officers do not like to stand outside in bad weather. By tomorrow night you have to be ready. Let's say 7pm. Astrid and me, we are going to pick you up at the Fountain."

Astrid who had kept silent, adds, "Finn, only take the most necessary things because we won't have much space for luggage." She looks at him in a way that tells Finn enough to know her desires and aspiration. He feels something strange going on with his stomach and has the idea that he is shrinking from tall to small, ending up fainting and becoming invisible in front of everyone. Being conscious to his body sensation and his emotions of shame, fear and nervousness, he straightens himself in his chair and says, "You guys have no idea what I am going through here. I prefer to leave sooner rather than later." And he throws an affectionate look to Astrid who responds to this attentive loving and flirting way by shining like a diamond. Had she not been taken by this illusion of romantic longing to be loved she would have noticed Finn's insecurity and would have heard the tiny inauthentic tones in his voice. She was in this soap bubble called romantic love. With this way of looking at things she was unable to get Finn's true intentions because she was too busy projecting hers onto him.

Finn and Bernd understood each other from the first moment they had met and seen each other. No further explanations necessary. Everything was obvious! Clear as crystal and flowing like water. They understood the needs of each other and from where they lived up to the values and principles of their lives.

Wow! Finn crept out of the boot of Bernd's car. Astrid and Bernd had been driving throughout the whole night. It was still dark outside when they stopped at the fuel station in the neighbourhood of Kempten on their way to Hamburg. Everything went as Bernd had planned. Coming outside of the fuel station they saw two men getting out of a car, walking straight in their direction. Finn froze and was ready to run. But Astrid turned around to kiss him passionately! Bernd, not showing any panic, asked them calmly for a light. One of the two pulled a lighter out of his trouser pocket and handed it to him. Bernd looked them directly into their faces, nodded attentively and continued on his way. Astrid had disappeared with Finn towards the toilets. From there they ran to the car where Finn disappeared into the boot of the car. Later on the motorway, when they had got rid of their fear and started to relax a little, they stopped the car to get Finn out of the boot.

By the silence of the night and the billions of glittering stars which appeared at the firmament of the universe, Finn got in touch with a deep sensation of peace and unconditional love. At this specific moment of time it seemed as if the cosmos proved its glory and as if it had sent a sign of anticipation of Finn's victory. Just for one moment they all experienced the holiness of the Universe which connects all people in the whole world. The certainty that there is one love in here and out there, became evident.

When Finn went with Astrid to the lawyer he got reminded of his escape from Italy. Astrid had taken him to her flat, a very decent place in a small town called Grohne close to the Dutch border. Astrid's sister had rented an apartment for her and had put some pieces of furniture into it. He felt at home. He felt comfortable, free and safe. Astrid had looked for work temporarily to support them financially while she continued working on her doctoral project. He was not supposed to leave the house before Astrid had investigated everything concerning his application for a permanent stay. It was not wise for him to leave the house without having been registered as a possible refugee.

The only contact he had besides Astrid and the TV was Bernd who called him. During these phone calls Bernd advised him to find his way to the authorities and to register as a Nigerian, seeking asylum in Germany as a persecuted homosexual. He feels bad about it because he is told to share it with no one. He has to lie once more to keep himself safe. Bernd, who had realized that Finn was gay, makes it his job to help him with going through his own process.

Astrid is busy demanding to stay with a partner which appears as a possibility.

Finn is very grateful. Only Bernd sees the stress and fear in Finn's eyes.

From the beginning he has noticed that Finn is a homosexual. He encourages Finn to start a story about himself, based on these facts. Meanwhile Finn plays the faithful lover and fiancé of Astrid. He invents lots of sweet romantic moments to please Astrid. They talk a lot, cuddle, he gives her fantastic massages and always waits with an interesting African dish to serve her when she comes back from work. She could not have dreamt of a better mate.

One day, they go to see the lawyer together. They meet a young, friendly and competent Dutch lady. He observes how she shows empathy and respect towards her clients. He decides to visit her once alone to talk about his problem. Perhaps he could even empty his heavy heart about the two stories he is in. The day they consult the lawyer he meets another Nigerian who is by himself and who complains that the authorities intend to send him back. He has learned German and has found work as a highly qualified engineer. His enterprise supports him against the authority, but they say the Dublin law has to be applied because the country he arrived in first is Italy. It is there where they have taken his fingerprints. Luckily Finn has never registered nor had his fingerprints taken in Italy. Otherwise by Dublin law his application for an A status would be rejected.

An Indian summer is what they call the sunny autumn days. When the light sparkles softly in the air, reflecting lovely autumn colours of yellow, brown, ochre, and a mix of different greens from meadow green, to bottle green, to petrol coloured landscapes and dark red Canadian leaves falling down from trees crowding pavements. Finn loves this time of year very much. The light is soft and caresses his face. It is not as hot as the summer months. As an African, he detests the heat.

Walking through the streets he imagines himself as a film director. A stay in Germany could make his dreams come true. In Africa he had written manuscripts and imagined film scenarios. His closest friends were artists and he, who had to earn his living as a taxi driver, understood that he had artistic talent and an abundance of creativity. At school he was fond of imagining and writing stories and poetry. His father was strictly against an artistic career and wanted him to become an accountant. That seemed to be a decent profession and a realistic one because he always complained about Finn being a dreamer.

When he arrived in Germany the snow was the biggest surprise. He had never been in the snow. He loved to dress himself warm, wearing ski clothes and ski underwear that kept his body warm. It took him a few weeks to realize that he had now arrived in a country where he can make his visions and dreams come true. He had finally arrived in a place where freedom and dignity of human rights were respected. The attractive lawyer advised him to keep both stories going. It was for his own security. She encourages him to think always first for himself, but he finds himself an egocentric, immoral man who exploited the kindness and innocence of a loving white woman. He is not a stand for himself. Instead, he blames and invalidates himself permanently. "Finn. Look what a corrupt, selfish guy you have become, a real bastard," he tells himself. Your mother would not like to hear that you have become - a cheater, a betrayer." He could not look anymore into her eyes. He feels immensely ashamed!

Walking through the streets of Grohne, watching the children playing outside, he makes up his mind to tell Astrid the truth about himself. He is scared to death. How would she take it? Could they stay connected as pure friends? It is his wish not to lose Astrid as a friend.

Finn has called her at her work to ask her to meet him in town. He proposes to have dinner and afterwards go to the cinema together. When they enter the Greek restaurant and take a seat opposite each other his stomach is paining him a lot.

"My sweetheart, how was your day?"

"Good, but also tiresome. I had to finish a lot of tasks and felt miserable the whole afternoon." Astrid looks pale. He has not observed her for a long period of time, being busy with this bullshit, his own story. He was so exhausted.

She replies, "I've been wanting to tell you something very exciting for a very long time, but I hesitated. You seemed to be very busy with yourself and you had to get acclimatised to Germany. That's why I haven't yet shared some spectacular news with you."

Finn shouts out "What precisely do you mean? Baby what are you talking about?"

He looks at Astrid and sees her cheeks are getting red. "Are you carrying a secret around with you, my dear?"

Astrid replies enthusiastically, "Yes, Finn I do!" Imagine, you are soon going to become a father. I am eight weeks pregnant and I am so happy for both of us."

Finn freezes! What, he a father? He never could have dreamed to become a father. Oh no! Not that! What a deception for Astrid! He closes his eyes asking God to help him out of this dilemma. Right at this moment Astrid gets a telephone call from Bernd. Astrid shares her being pregnant with him and he asks her: "How does Finn like this news?"

"Why", Astrid replies! "of course, he is happy."

"It is his child?" Bernd insists and advises her to ask Finn. After having finished the call she says, "Bernd wants to know if you like me being pregnant."

Finn finally takes courage to open up by sharing his secret about being gay. How he hates himself for deceiving her, for lying and for getting her pregnant. Astrid does not know what to say. She is speechless. "What! You are not heterosexual?"

"No Astrid, I am gay!"
"What do you mean?" Astrid screams loudly. "So you did it without any feelings?" Astrid questions him nervously.

"No not necessarily. I carry unconditional love for you in my heart. You know, don't you?" Finn continues without making eye contact. Astrid is unable to answer.

Astrid screams loudly. She jumps up to leave the restaurant in a hurry. Finn runs after her. They go home. There is an indescribable silence.

At home Astrid goes directly to her room and calls her best friend. She does not turn up in their common sleeping room. Finn cannot sleep! Next week he will certainly have to move out to another apartment.

However, the following day, to his surprise, Astrid greets him in a friendly way and seems to be in excellent humour. "Finn. It is up to you. You will have to choose! Do you want to stay and raise our child together with me? It will be a win - win situation. You will become a father and I will get a child. We would both share the house, the duties and live our friendship."

"But will it work for you?" Finn asks.

Astrid answers "Yes, why not? I don't want to lose you as a friend and as the father of my child. We will raise it together perhaps with the help of a boyfriend or two? What fun! I will be surrounded by men. Let's hope that the baby won't be a boy!"

Finn says "Astrid, we gays are different to hetero. We are more like girls. We can feel more feminine. Do you know that?"

"Yeah", Astrid laughs "That's right! The world should become more feminine. Then we would live peacefully without violence or greediness. The planet could become a brilliant place to live. Mother earth can get its power and beauty back."

"What name should we give our daughter?"
"Wait, wait! It can be a boy!" Finn laughs. "Okay, let's choose a male and female name then."
"And a German and a Nigerian one," Finn adds.
"All right! What do you think about Felix? That means the happy one." Astrid smiles all over her face and she says cheekily, "Or Felicia?"

On their way home he looks at the people who are in the street heading towards a club or a cinema to watch a film, or being out to have some fun on a Friday night. He is in a world where he is supposed to make himself become a foreigner, a refugee. He does not have friends and does not speak their language yet. Will he become familiar with these people who differ from him? Will he be able to adapt to their strange habits? Will they like him and accept and respect him, or will he become one of the lonely ones who start isolating and surrounding themselves with people from their own culture, rather than integrating?

An inner conviction spreads through his veins and he says silently to himself: "Finn, you are on a journey. Enjoy the challenges and see life as a big adventure where you are a warrior making your dreams come true."

Doug Dunn

In 2017, I moved to Devon from East London and retired from full-time work as a Software Trainer. Connecting with the community through tennis, bridge and astronomy, I started treating retirement as my new career. As well as taking up committee work for a local community trust, I started volunteering for the National Trust. For much of 2018, I became a Facilitator for a Landmark Worldwide course called Wisdom Unlimited.[ii]

Joining the Writers Empowerment Club in 2017, run by Noha Nasser, led me into several writing projects: joining a local creative writing class, submitting two reports for a published journal for Landmark's Conference for Global Transformation in 2018 and 2019, and republishing a sci-fi short story 'Being On The Moon' through Kindle Direct Publishing.

My story 'The New Jungle Project' expresses the resilience of refugees and volunteers in Calais and my stand for people to live wherever they want to, including on the moon! 'Crossing from India' is about my parent's immigration to the UK and me discovering the gift of mixed race identity.

Crossing from India

(Photo credit: unsplash.com)

My parents immigrated to the United Kingdom from India in 1958 when I was almost two years old. I have always considered myself to be British having no memories of India and having never been back. When people hear me say this, they are usually surprised. They often say how wonderful their visit to India was and how much they love the country. Thanks to joining the Human Crossings group, where I have learned about refugees, my attitude is changing.

The dictionary defines a refugee as a person who has been forced to leave their country in order to escape war, persecution or natural disaster. An immigrant is a person who comes to live permanently in a foreign country while an emigrant is a person leaving from their country to settle in another. A migrant is a person who moves from one place to another, especially to find work or better working conditions.

Last year I became friends with Khaled, a refugee from Syria. I was touched and moved by his determination, openness and bravery on the journey he made to Lebanon and finally Exeter. He never gave up. When living in Lebanon he found ways to overcome dangers and challenges and when the opportunity came to cross to the United Kingdom he was ready to make it happen. Now Khaled and his family connect and integrate fully with the local community though many volunteering activities.

Hearing Khaled's story made me think about my parents 60 years ago; how brave and determined they must have been to uproot and travel thousands of miles from India to start a new life in the United Kingdom. They lived in Calcutta within a social group called 'Anglo-Indians'. They were of mixed origin dating back several generations. The Anglo-Indian community were employed by the British for administrative work in the civil service, on the railways and in medical professions. My grandfather on my mother's side was chairman of the East Indian Railways, a leader within the 'Railway people'. They lived in the Railway Colony, a neatly kept oasis away from the heat, noise and bustle of India.[iii] They enjoyed being part of the Railway Institute, being part British, and didn't like to think of themselves as Indian.

My Dad died in 2003 and my Mum in 2004. It was very sudden and I miss hearing their stories about life in India. When I spoke to my sister recently she suggested I watch the TV programme 'Passage To Britain'[iv] and read 'Bhowani Junction'[v] to get a sense of Anglo-Indian society in the mid 1940s prior to Indian independence. My brother reminded me that Mum and Dad had to make a choice between staying in India and becoming Indian or leaving and becoming British. Both choices had uncertain futures. My father would have to give up a well-paid career as an electrical engineer and start again, retaking exams in a foreign country. But they decided that leaving India was the right choice for the sake of our education. My brother, in a visit to India, met some Anglo-Indians who chose to stay. They became child minders for local schools. But it is impossible to say how life would have turned out for my family.

We were luckier than many immigrants crossing from India. Analysis of passenger lists from ships sailing between Bombay and England shows that in the late 1940s passengers were mostly male Indians leaving to better their lives. Immigration from commonwealth countries was encouraged and jobs were plentiful in locations such as the West Midlands. They would earn in a week what would take a year to earn in India. They aimed to work hard, save money and send it back to their families and children in India.

In the 1950s the passenger lists show many more wives and children immigrating than earlier. My parents came in 1958 from Bombay on the P&O Strathaird. Their plan was to live in an area where there were few Asians. My father applied for work in the East Midlands while my mother waited in London with my brother and me. Dad was offered a job at Ericksons near Nottingham and soon they bought a semi-detached house in the village of Attenborough. My parents integrated with the community by attending events at the local village hall. Mum became an active Women's Institute member and Girl Guides leader.

So what am I getting from reading Bhowani Junction? From the first chapter I gained a better understanding of the Anglo-Indian mindset in the 1940s. The narrator, a railway traffic superintendent, says: 'Anglo-Indians couldn't become English, because we were half Indian. We couldn't become Indian, because we were half English. We could only stay where we were and be what we were. The English would go away now and leave us ...'

I started to see why my parents had no strong wish to return to India. They often said they wanted to remember India the way they left it.Looking back on my childhood I sometimes felt I wasn't wanted because I was different. That Anglo-Indian culture was still there in my background and now in adult life. I had relationships with English women and was married for 12 years but I put something in the way of creating totally loving and fulfilling relationships.

My ex-wife very kindly gave me another book about Anglo-Indians: 'The Anglo-Indians – A 500-Year History'. I enjoyed the book and was surprised to read that my father's brother Pat Dunn was one of four Anglo-Indians in the Indian Army who reached the rank of Lieutenant-General. He was the first Indian Colonel to command a battalion. Later in the book my mother's first cousin Monsignor Eric Barber is acknowledged for being bishop of Calcutta for several years. Reading this book made me feel proud of my family connections and being a part of the Anglo-Indian community.

Since participating on this refugee project I have become more accepting about being of a different culture. I finally like the colour of my skin! Asians are a bit of a rarity where I live in Devon, so often people are curious. I am starting to enjoy talking about India without sounding apologetic for not returning. My children are showing an interest in their background and we are talking about arranging a trip to India next year.

Recently, I gave a short talk with slides on 'Life Experiences' to a community group in my village hall about a volunteering trip I made to Malawi in 2018. The talk went well and afterwards I was asked to consider becoming a member of the local Activity Trust committee. My first thought was 'No, I'm too busy'. A few days later I was asked again by another person and rather than listening to my own internal thoughts I listened to the community. I said 'Yes' having come to terms with being different.

I am pleased to have introduced Khaled to the Human Crossings group. It's wonderful that he shares his experiences so openly with us. The project is allowing me to connect more with different cultures. I am finally starting to embrace my Indian background.

Pope Francis recently returned from a historic first-ever visit to the United Arab Emirates. Referring specifically to the wars in Yemen, Syria, Iraq and Libya, he told a gathering of religious leaders to reject every nuance of approval of the word 'war'. Another highlight was the signing of a document on human fraternity affirming freedom of beliefs which says: 'Human diversity including the pluralism and diversity of religions is willed by God. It includes the essential requirement to recognise the rights of women, and for the wealthy to care for the poor, destitute and marginalised. It calls on all concerned to stop using religion to incite hatred, violence and blind fanaticism.'

I was moved by what Pope Francis said. There should be no place in the world for hatred of religions or cultures.

Crossing from India was a challenge for my parents but also a gift for me; I have experienced starting life in a new country. Writing about refugees has opened my eyes to the one-sided view I have held as an Anglo-Indian and see the prejudices I have believed to be true. I am open to creating new relationships and embarking on new adventures.

The New Jungle Project

(Museum of the Moon. Photo credit: Doug Dunn)

I wrote this story after watching 'The Jungle'[vi] in London at the Young Vic in December 2017. The play depicted life in the refugee camp in Calais called 'The Jungle' by performers who actually lived there as refugees and volunteers. I watched the show with two people from my writers' group who were writing about refugees. At the end of the show we spoke with a few of the cast members in the bar. I was very touched by their openness and passion.

A few days later I was visiting my daughter in Sheffield and en route I stopped to visit the Museum of the Moon in Leicester.[vii] The cast members were still very much in my mind and I was often thinking about refugees. I wondered where next the cast members might be performing. I thought about their passion and what I am passionate about.

The most important passion in my life is astronomy and space travel. It has remained my biggest interest since I was five years old. I still vividly remember going to the Birthday party of Rory, a friend from school. At Rory's party his father gave everyone a piece of paper and a pencil and asked us to draw a picture of the pencil! While we were busy drawing, his father said we were about to go on a journey. We would be travelling by rocket up into space on a trip to the Moon! We finished our drawings and passed them round. They seemed to look more like space rockets to me than pencils. Then we all got up and went into the garden. It was dark and we were led into a shed shaped like a space rocket. When everyone was inside the door was closed and we suddenly heard banging and rumbling on the outside of the shed. We seemed to be moving and it felt like the shed was taking off. After a while it went quiet and the shed door opened. We had landed on the Moon! We all got out and had a lot of fun running around.

That memory has stayed with me. It was only a few years before the Apollo landings so people were talking a lot about space travel. How exciting it must be to actually travel to the Moon. Now, finally in 2017 people were again talking about space travel. Here, I was at a museum with many people talking about the Moon. I had the thought that those from 'The Jungle' show would have the perfect pioneering spirit for space travel. They were used to living in harsh conditions and in small closed communities. It would be wonderful to meet them again and ask what they thought of that idea.

"How amazing to see you again. Your show was so realistic. I loved it," I said to a one of 'The Jungle' cast members I spotted drinking coffee.

"Thank you. I remember talking with you in the bar," said Beth.

"I didn't expect to see you here!"

"Derek is passionate about astronomy and anything to do with space. He got us to come to this Science Week thing in Leicester," explained Beth.

"The model of the Moon is supposed to be spectacular," I said.

"Yes. We are about to go in. Hi I'm Derek. I remember you now."

Five members from the cast were there. The young English volunteer Beth, an Afghan refugee called Salar, a young English volunteer Sam, a refugee from West Sudan called Okot and Derek, a retired British volunteer.

I asked if I could join them in the museum. They seemed happy so we walked through the cathedral door past a tall poster entitled 'Museum of the Moon'. Before us was a huge bright sphere of the Moon. Seven meters across, suspended above our heads and looking very real.

"Very soon there will be people taking trips to the Moon. Elon Musk has a reusable spacecraft called Dragon ready to transport people on commercial space trips." Derek said pointing to one of the dark areas on the Moon's surface. "Here's where the Apollo astronauts landed in 1969. The Sea of Tranquillity."

We all walked up to take a closer look. "This side of the Moon always faces the Earth. Only a few people have actually seen the far side of the Moon. Come and take a look!" he said encouraging everyone to walk round the balloon.

"The surface looks so real," said Sam, smiling. "It makes me realise how small we are." Beth put her arm around Sam. They had worked together for over a year now and were becoming close.

Okot looked uneasily across at Sam and Beth. "I heard about men stepping on the Moon. But I didn't really believe it happened. Some say it is just a story."

"I know," said Derek, putting his arm on Okot's shoulder. "When you see the Moon shining at night it's hard to believe astronauts have been up there. Wouldn't it be great for people to be living up on the Moon?"

Some people were reading a display poster. It said this installation was created by the artist Luke Jerram and named Museum of the Moon. It had been touring the UK and Europe for the past two years. It was simply a large helium balloon with a light inside. On its surface was printed high-resolution photographic data obtained from NASA.

"Thank you for inviting us here Derek. It was such a surprise!" said Beth.

"It made me feel like an astronaut orbiting round," said Sam.

"I had no idea people are going on Moon trips," said Salar. "Some people have more money than brains."
"I agree. Who can afford to spend millions on a one week trip?" said Beth.

"I'm hoping the flight fare will come down in the future," replied Derek. "Everything is happening so quickly. Before long, there will be a people living on the Moon."

"Do you think people are ready to live on the Moon?" I asked. "Do you think people will be able to live together in such a close community?"

"No. I don't think they will be," replied Salar.

"I think a lot of research needs to happen before they let people live in space," said Sam.

"What kind of research? What problems do you think people need to look at?" Derek asked.

I was pleased Derek was asking questions.

"Food research" said Salar. "How to grow and make it."

"Water" said Okot, the young refugee from West Sudan.

"Sanitation!" said Beth. "How to dispose of waste."

"Yes. Let's not have land fill on the Moon. We must keep it as clean as possible." Sam said. "How about crime? How would they deal with fighting or bad behaviour?"

Salar laughed. "This reminds me of our weekly elders meetings. They could have the same sort of problems we had in The Jungle."

"I agree with you Salar," I said. "You all have useful community-building skills."

"We missed one. What about sex?" asked Beth. "I think there could be some big problems on the Moon around that subject!"

"That might be true. All these things could be looked at and discussed before people go there."

"Yes they should. There was no planning before The Jungle. It just happened as we went along," said Salar.

"Perhaps that's why it didn't last," said Derek. "We didn't know there would be so many migrants. There was no pre-planning."

"That's right. But I'm sure 'migration' to the Moon will eventually happen and maybe sooner than we think. So, what can we do before they start sending people up there?" I went to the café to buy a few snacks. When I returned, everyone was laughing.

"We think they should build a community here first," said Sam.

"Yes," said Salar. "We think a group of about 20 people and from different countries would be good. With the common language being English."

Beth said, "Sam and I would like to volunteer for the new community. Salar said he would if he can grow and cook food. Okot doesn't believe we have actually been to the Moon. But he still wants to come!"

"Brilliant!" I said. "Let's go with your idea. Where should we locate our camp? What do you think about building again in Calais?"

"No way!" said Beth. "I hate the French. I would never want to go back to that place."

"I agree," said Sam. "I still have nightmares about that time the bulldozers came."

"I know you don't want to return to Calais," I said. "That must have been the worst night of your lives when the camp was closed down. To see your home being pulled down. Hundreds of migrants still gather there. Returning and setting up another camp there would be a great way of remembering the work you did. A kind of legacy to The Jungle. Perhaps we could call it 'The New Jungle'."

"That sounds good," said Derek. "But the French government won't be interested. The President said he wants no more homeless migrants in the woods."

"They are unlikely to support a permanent camp," said Sam.

"Derek. Would you be willing to act as our news contact person?" I asked. "I think the French President is keen to create something new and inspiring around the refugee issue."
"Sure. I'll keep a log of news articles and social media posts." Derek always liked to keep up with the news and keep people informed.

"Start by writing a letter to the President. We should invite him to a meeting where we propose our plan," I said.

"Are you serious? What plan? We don't really have one", said Beth.

The Plan

"I would suggest we work backwards from where we end up. Some people say it's the best way to plan a project." I learned this on a course for team management and leadership[viii]. We would stand at the point where the project is fulfilled and look back at the steps or milestones that got us there.

"There will be a time when thousands of people will be living on the Moon. That might be in 50 years time. What would have to happen in 10 years' time?" I asked.

Sam said, "Sending the first group of people to live up there."

"Ok. This is just a rough plan. We can adjust the numbers depending on how the project develops. How many people?"

"Salar thought 20. There should be many different skills. Some scientists, engineers, doctors, geologist", said Beth.

"Cooks," said Salar. "And, of course, people to grow the food."

"Good. So what needs to happen in five years for those 20 people to have safely landed and be living together?" I asked.

"Well," offered Derek, "they would have had to complete building a space camp. Then test the equipment and infrastructure. And make or transport everything they will need."

"They could use drones doing some of the work," said Sam smiling at the thought of robots on the Moon.

"Yes they would use robots for building. It would need to start well before. Let's say in two or three years' time," I said.

"Before that they would need to choose a suitable location." Derek suggested. "So what should we be thinking about in the next two years?"

"I guess we should practise living together in a camp similar to the one for the Moon," said Beth. "Everyone needs to learn how to get on. As we found

174

in Calais, it doesn't work to be separate. Better to work as a body where everyone matters and contributes to the life in the camp."

"That's great, Beth and everyone. As you say, we should be making the most of our time now." I said. "You guys are quick thinking and very inventive. You bounce ideas off each other. Unfortunately, we don't have a camp right now to practise living together. This will come if the French Government sees something valuable in what we are doing, hopefully if we can arrange a meeting with their President. But what can we do right now?"

"Nothing," said Salar "until we have a place to go."

"We can talk," said Derek "like we are doing right now."

"Talk is cheap," said Okot. "We need actions rather than talk."

"So I have a suggestion," I said, "till we have the backing to build a new camp."

"If we get the backing," said Beth.

"My suggestion is that we meet through video conferencing once a week. All you need is a laptop. Each week we discuss a new topic."

"What about our meeting with the government?" Asked Sam.

"That's true," said Beth. "We were going to have a meeting. I know. Let's invite the French President to our next meeting!"

"He's far too busy for that," said Okot. "He probably has a full schedule for the next two years."

"Plans change. I think he has quite a lot of say about his plans," I said. "His idea to loan the Bayeux Tapestry to Britain seemed to come out of the blue, didn't it?"

"You're right. It was the first time this was done in 950 years," said Derek. "Also his policy on refugees is becoming more flexible. This might be a good time for a new initiative."

"Ok let's do it. Are we all agreed?" Beth looked around and everyone put up their hands apart from Salar.

"What's the matter Salar? Do you not agree?" Asked Sam.

"I don't like these video calls. There is no chance to share food."

"Yes. You guys can still meet and make some nice food during the sessions. In fact, it is better to be in a small group," I said.

"I see," said Salar, smiling. "So if I can cook I'm in! When shall we have the first meeting?"

"Brilliant!" said Beth. "We are all agreed. What's the topic for our first meeting?"

Meeting 1 - Language

The next day I sent an email invitation to the New Jungle team members. The topic to discuss would be Language. I acknowledged the group for being bold and adventurous and said that one day they will be seen as pioneers. They may become our first migrants crossing into space. I said there might be times when they forget they are bold pioneers and that it is important to remember why we are doing this. The reason why I was doing this was because I believed every human being has the right to travel wherever they want on our planet.

At the end of the email I asked everyone to think about this question: "Which language or languages should people speak on the Moon?"

The first meeting was going to be very exciting. As well as our group of six, the French President confirmed he would attend part of the meeting.

"Hi Beth. Welcome!" I said. I could see Sam and Salar on the laptop screen with Beth.

"Salam! Look at the food we have here. It is like the Good Chance cafe all over again," said Salar standing in his kitchen.
I waved at the screen."Great to see you all again."

Derek and Okot appeared on the screen in separate windows.

"Hi Derek. Thank you for joining us. Hello Okot. Good to see you are all connected. Before we start, does anyone have any guests?" I asked.

"Yes," said Derek, "the French President said he would join us 30 minutes into the meeting."

"Really! That is perfect. Well done Derek for making that happen," I said. "So let's get started. Which language should we speak on the Moon? Who would like to share? Just raise a hand if you'd like to speak then click the microphone icon to unmute yourself. Yes Beth."

"I guess English, as it is so widely spoken."
"The most common language in the world is Chinese," said Okot.

"He's right. Over a billion people speak Mandarin," added Derek. "But it's not an easy language for Westerners. Spanish is the second most common language and I think English is third."
"So we shouldn't assume it will be English. It also depends on other things. For instance, are there going to be countries and borders on the Moon?" I asked.

Everyone put up their hands. "Yes Beth, then Sam."

"No," said Beth emphatically. "Definitely no borders. Many are man-made and they just cause conflict. Birds migrate and live quite happily without borders!"

"That is true about birds. Though they have territories," added Sam.

Beth stared at Sam for disagreeing with her.

"You're right, Beth," said Sam. "Birds seem to manage well enough without making borders."

"It is interesting that many species of birds migrate huge distances every year. We can probably learn a lot from them," I said. "I think the languages spoken will depend on which countries are first to go into space. But let's not fight over this issue. One day it may not be an issue at all as we might have excellent voice translator technology."

I noticed a hand raised. "Yes, Salar."

"In The Jungle we often spoke English with each other. It was a big problem for the French."
"Thank you for raising that Salar. No one wanted to speak or learn French. How was that for you guys?" I asked.

"We wanted to get to the UK," replied Okot, "so why would we want to learn French?"

"That's true. I know school French but get stuck when French people ask me a question," said Beth.

"Me too," agreed Sam.

"It is difficult to learn a new language," said Derek, "especially for us English."

178

"So how do you think that was for the French police and the government reps that came to the camp?" I asked.

"They knew we weren't going to stay in France. I don't know why they got upset," said Beth.

Salar said, "I think they got upset because we didn't care about them."

"Thank you Salar. You guys didn't care. Anything else?"

"We didn't like them," admitted Sam.

"Is that how it was?"

"We hated them!" said Beth. "I don't know why. We hated it when the police or officials came. It was like they were the enemy. It was us and them."

"It's good to see how it was. Owning up to how it was allows us to move forward." I said. "Sounds like there was no communication between The Jungle members and the police. I wonder how you seemed to them."

Everyone was quiet.

"How would you feel if a group of people hated you?"

"I'd hate them back. It would be horrible," said Derek.

"I didn't really think of that. I was thinking only of what we could get for the refugees," said Beth. "But now I realize they must have been pretty pissed off!"

"They must have been. And probably still are," I said.

At that moment, a new person appeared on the screen. It was the French President.

"Welcome Monsieur President! Derek said you would be joining us." I said. "Some of the people here were members of The Jungle camp two years ago."

"Thank you for inviting me. I will try to speak in English. I am interested to hear why you have met up again. Derek has given me a quick briefing. Please continue with your discussion," the President said encouragingly.

"Well to be honest, we were just saying how The Jungle residents felt about the French and how we thought you might have felt about us," I said.

"Très intéressant! How did you feel about each other?"

"Well Monsieur President. To be frank we really hated each other!" Beth said jokingly.

"I know this. And it is something that has been of great concern and disappointment."

"I think what developed from the breakdown in communication was what is termed dehumanization." I said. "The police saw The Jungle group as a thing rather than a community of people. Less than human. Similar to how slaves were once thought of by their owners."

"That's true," said Derek. "They thought of us as animals in a jungle. But the volunteers also dehumanized the French. We thought of them as aggressive thugs."

"It's totally understandable. When two groups refuse to relate to each other as human beings, they start dehumanising each other. It has happened throughout history resulting in thousands of wars, slavery, and racism. It's quite normal!"I said, smiling.

"Wasn't this meeting actually about language? What conclusions did you reach?" asked the President.

"Hello sir. My name is Salar. Chef of the Good Chance Café in the Jungle. I think we should have cared more about learning the French language."

"Yes. We did avoid doing that. We needed someone like you!" said Sam.

"Thank you Sam. French people were not included in the network of the Jungle camp. A way to do that might have been having French classes as well as English classes in the camp."

"Perhaps we could have had interpreters," suggested Beth. "That would have helped with communication."

"Good point. I will include that in the project plan," I said. "Derek mentioned we have a project to prepare and train people for living on the Moon. We thought the former Jungle site would be a good location. The purpose of the camp is to test equipment and research social protocols. See how people get on in a small closed community. NASA calls it a Moon Analog Habitat."

"Sounds interesting," said the President. "Where's the funding coming from for this project?"

"NASA has started doing this but their initiative is long term," I said. "I am inviting Elon Musk to our next session to discuss commercial funding of our camp.

"The topic of the next session is Money. Thank you all for attending today. We have agreed that we are not going to let the language we speak cause issues. Eventually there will probably be many communities speaking different languages on the Moon. Being smaller than Earth may encourage people to learn the languages of their neighbours.

"Before the next session have a think about this question:

Would it be possible to live in a world without money?

"See you all next week!"

Beth's group continued chatting together after the meeting. She clicked the 'leave meeting' link on the screen. "Pass the naan bread Sam. This curry is perfect."

"Thank you. It is my pleasure to cook for you again. It brings back great memories," said Salar placing a pot of goat meat curry on his table.

"This is so good to be hanging out again," said Sam. "And with the others. Seeing them on that big screen was so real."

"I know. It's like they are here with us," said Beth sitting close to Sam. "Come on Salar. Group hug!"

Since leaving The Jungle, Beth and Sam had been doing their own thing. Both were still coming to terms with the dismantling of the camp. It was hard for both of them to move on.

"I love it that we have come together again," said Beth.

"Yes," agreed Sam. "With a purpose. I don't know right now how going to the Moon will help refugees but I'm willing to go along with it."

"I agree," said Salar holding up a glass of wine. "I am inspired. I think my people in Afghanistan will be inspired. It is a good idea."

Meeting 2 - Money

"Hi everyone," I said. "Welcome to our meeting session two. I hope you all had a great week." It was 19:00 CET and everyone in the team showed up on the screen. "Thank you for dialling in on time.

"So the question I left you with to consider was – Would it be possible to live in a world without money? Who would like to share? Yes Beth, then Derek then Okot."

"I did think about this," said Beth. "Some of my parents' friends lived on a Kibbutz in Israel where they had virtually no money. It was back in the 80s and young guys from all over the world worked together as volunteers.

They were paid 20 shekels a week, which just about covered their cigarettes. Food was home-grown and plentiful and everyone lived rent-free. The system seemed to work."

"I was one of those volunteers in Israel back in 1985," said Derek. "It was hard work but there was time to relax and rest. Even party! What I remember was that the resident Kibbutzniks seemed to have money. They started buying coloured TVs and expensive clothes. It became a kind of status thing, I think."

"Thank you Derek," I said. "So in your experience, life without money worked for the volunteers but not for some of the permanent members of the community. Okot, did you want to add anything?"

"It would be interesting to hear about money in your country, Sudan," I said.

"Yes, Darfur in the west of Sudan," said Okot. "I say money causes trouble. People who have it control those who don't. I think it is better to live without money."

"Have you ever been in a place where money is not used?" I asked.

"Yes. When my mother was alive, she took me to visit my uncle in Malawi. I love those times. My uncle is a farmer growing maize and tobacco. Most people there are farmers earning very little money. But it is a good life."

"Yes, Malawi is based mainly on agriculture. But surely the farmers must have money to buy and sell?" I asked.

"Most people there don't have bank accounts. Some use Mobile Money[ix]," said Okot.

"Mobile Money? What is that, Okot?" asked Beth.

"More people have mobile phones than bank accounts. It is a good way to make safe payments by phone. It is very fast and easy. I can show you, if you like," said Okot holding up his phone.

"That's ok. I like the idea of by-passing bank accounts," I said.

"It's quite an advanced technology," Derek said. "Sometimes third world countries embrace new technologies before they become adopted in countries from the First World. I think it's a case of 'needs must'."

"Perhaps we should adopt the same method at the camp. It may be a way of making payments out in space via satellites," Sam said. "I've been reading a book called Ubuntu by Michael Tellinger[x]. He describes how money and banks have for a long time totally controlled our lives."

"I read that too," said Beth. "It says if we change our thinking and dependence on money we would only need to work for three hours a week."

"Really! Three hours a week? That sounds like utopia." Salar said.

"I was surprised, too. But it is not utopia according to the author. There would be a natural order of things if we aren't corrupted by money. His plan is for people to live in small rural towns and produce a surplus of food. This could be achieved with every person contributing just three hours of their time each week to rural work."

"So what do people do with the rest of the week?" asked Salar. "I would have so much time for cooking."

"I wrote some notes from the Ubuntu Contributionism idea," said Beth. "Tellinger says 'each individual is encouraged to follow their passion and contribute their natural talents or acquired skills to the greater benefit of all the community. Everyone's contribution would be treated as equally and infinitely valuable'."

Sam also read out from his notebook. "And his Five Point Mantra is: No money, no barter, no trade, no value attached to anything that makes it more valuable than anything else, and everyone contributes their natural talents or acquires skills for the greater benefit of the community."

"Sam and I decided to read Ubuntu this week and share about it at this meeting," said Beth.
"Great work. You've made a useful contribution."
"It is a good example of Contributionism," joked Sam.

"Yes it is! I especially want to acknowledge Beth and Sam for working together on reviewing the Ubuntu ideas."

Beth waved her hand to share. "Thank you. Actually, we have a bit of an announcement to make. Last week Sam proposed to me! It was such a surprise. We've only been officially going out for two weeks."

"Yes but we were in Calais for over a year," said Sam.

"That's true," Beth added. "We have been through a lot together."

"So what did you say? I hope it was yes!" asked Salar.

"It was yes, Salar. We don't have a date planned, as yet, but we're now engaged. I am so happy. He even gave me a ring." Beth put her hand close to the laptop camera so everyone could see.

"That's so beautiful. How lovely that you are together," I said. "Thank you for attending today everyone. See you at the next meeting, which strangely is about sex! How will people handle sex on the Moon?"

Meeting 3 – Sex on the Moon

So much had happened since the previous meeting. Not only had Sam and Beth got engaged but also the French President gave the go ahead for the New Jungle Project. Funding came jointly from SpaceX and the European Space Agency following an announcement the week before that China was to launch a manned lunar mission to the far side of the Moon in 2020. Construction of a new building was underway at the Calais distribution centre and a temporary Portacabin with basic utilities was provided for the project team. Rather than having an online conference, everyone attended Meeting 3 in the project cabin in Calais.

I started the meeting. "I'm pleased you adjusted your schedules to be here. Sorry it is so cramped. The new building will be ready for use in a month's time. We will have twice as much room and much better seats."

"How exciting!" exclaimed Beth. "We will have our own camp. Yes these plastic chairs are not that comfy. How did all this happen?"

"I think it was a bit of luck having the China initiative. And sharing our meetings online really helped to promote our project. It's good that everyone seems to want to go to the Moon right now.

"You might be wondering why on earth we are discussing a topic like sex. People don't normally do that. Well, we won't be on Earth and it won't be a normal situation. The other question to ask is; should we be making babies on the Moon? Or should we wait until a community is sufficiently developed? What I thought might work is to discuss these in pairs and then share as a group."

Beth and Sam started sharing straight away. This was something they had already talked about. "I think it is important to talk about this. Don't you, Sam?" asked Beth.

"Kind of. But it feels a bit weird."

"I know. But suppose we decided to go to the Moon, say next year. It definitely feels weird saying this. Then suppose I got pregnant, would we want to have our baby up there?"

"I guess it depends on risk. If they have all the medical stuff needed for childbirth I say have our baby in space. It would be the first space baby."

"We are just talking hypothetically. We only got engaged last week! I would like to be married first. But definitely, if there was adequate equipment provided. As for sex on the Moon, I'm all for it!" said Beth.

"It is an interesting question for people not in a relationship," said Sam. "It would be like people on an expedition or in the armed forces. If people had partners on Earth then they should be able to return home every few months."

"That's a good point Sam," I said. "People there should be able to take leave time whether they have partners or not. Every three months to stay in touch with family and for health reasons to strengthen muscles."

Salar had paired up with Okot. Both were looking uncomfortable by this topic. "I don't think we should be talking about these sorts of questions. If God wants people to have a family it will happen."

"In Sudan women don't talk about such things," said Okot.

"Please can you tell us more Okot," Salar said.

"In the capital city Juba, girls can be married at 10 years old. Some are bought in exchange for cows, then violently abused. Most violence is by partners in their home. When the civil war started in Darfur, there were rapes and genital mutilations happening all the time. The women were afraid to speak up in case they were tried for adultery." Okot started to cry as he remembered how his mother was gang raped by army soldiers in a forest.

"Sorry to hear that. It's hard for us to understand," said Salar.

"I don't think people here understand. We never talked about sex. We didn't have what people in the West have," said Okot.

"We are the same," said Salar. "In Afghanistan we have a 'three time abuse' rule. If a woman is abused by her partner, on the third time elders allow a divorce to take place. But many abuses are not reported. It is very difficult to discuss topics like sex or having children. Many are just trying to survive and avoid being abused or killed. They are not used to discussing anything."

Derek paired up with me to discuss the questions. "To be honest, I feel embarrassed discussing the first question. I am from a generation where such matters are not talked about directly. I think sex is a private matter for the community members to decide."

"Yes. I am from the same generation. Though we did live through the 60s and 70s," I said, thinking back to those days. "It is a private matter for the community. But if we are the community, it would be worth thinking about it."

"Well. If we have medical people and equipment why not have babies," said Derek. "It might be best to return to Earth once or twice a year for health checks. So in that case, yes to sex."

"I agree. There is also an opportunity to look at how we think about sex. Rather than the images we get from films, TV and pornography, we could discover new ways to talk about sexuality."

"That sounds interesting. What are you thinking of?"

"We know many disciplines have studied sexuality though the ages. It's a huge subject. But people might find new ways of expressing sexuality. A practice called Orgasmic Meditation[xi] may become popular. The 'OM' practice enables men to give orgasms to women in a non-sexual way. The practice might work in a small closed community and lessen the need for coupling up."

After the exercise, people shared and everyone agreed it was a useful talk. It was good to see how people had very widely different views and experiences. Beth and Sam were excited about being the first couple to start a family in space. We all agreed it is important to have access to a medical facility on the Moon.

Weekly meetings continued to be well attended and became a productive part of the New Jungle project. It helped keep the team focussed on one issue at a time. The topics for discussion were often suggested by team members and they took it in turns to lead meetings.

Moving into the new base building was very exciting. The group enjoyed imagining they were actually on the Moon carrying out tasks as if they were in the lunar environment. It was difficult at first relating to each other without social media or any personal computers. But people learned new ways of engaging. The discussion about sex seemed to become popular. It was like being volunteers on a remote campsite. Everyone enjoyed wearing spacesuits outside the base as it reminded them of why they were there. There was a lot of fun and laughter, and any major upsets or disagreements were cleared up at the weekly meetings.

After a few weeks, new people were introduced to the group and a second base was constructed to accommodate the additional community members. The aim was to increase numbers to 20 people willing to take the next step, to go to the Moon. Only those who were sure were accepted. With the apparent success of the New Jungle Project several other countries followed suit. A new initiative was to have at least one person from every country to live on the Moon.

As planned, the first few space launches were for constructing the Luna Base infrastructure. New techniques were implemented using solar mirrors to melt lunar rocks and form building materials. People from every country became captivated by watching the rapid progress of construction on the

189

Moon. As happened with the Apollo 11 landing, the whole world were united and had a part in the project of living on the Moon.

Time soon came for the first human launches and landings to take place. Within just a few years space travel became almost as common as air flight. Travelling to the Moon became 'normal' and interest rapidly developed into exploring other destinations of our Solar System including Mars and some of the satellites of Jupiter and Saturn. Human Beings were exploring space, together.

50 Years Later

Many people are now living on the Moon. People on Earth look up at the night sky and see the Moon in a new way. They see more than a rocky grey sphere in the night sky. They know that fellow humans are living up there enjoying a new way of life; living without borders, money, guns or drugs; showing what is possible both on the Moon and on Earth. How inspiring it is to know we are living on a second world. The Moon is a shining example of how life can be.

Refugees could play an important part in this adventure. Their bravery and pioneering spirit is an inspiration. Many humans will make the crossing into space, some to the Moon and some to moons of other planets. Some will return and remind us how beautiful and rich our planet is. They show us how anything is possible when we work together with a common purpose.

Acknowledgements

In the making of this book, first and foremost I want to give a big thank you to the eight authors who volunteered their time and energy. Especially to Khaled who shared his journey from Syria with us and then wrote it out in Arabic. Thank you Dr Alaa Nasser for kindly translating Khaled's story into English.

In particular we thank Noha Nasser for managing the project and empowering group members to contribute in different ways. It has been a pleasure working together. A special thanks also to our editor Stephen Terry for skilfully rearranging sentences and turning our text into a readable whole. Thank you Stephen for writing the Foreword and contributing greatly to the project.

We also thank other authors who initially signed up but could not complete with us for one reason or another; Zoe Gilhirst, Heather Salmon, Saci Kumara Nimai Das, Clarissa Kasasa, Farida Kasasa, and Raquel Maria. Your encouragement and involvement, no matter how short or long, was appreciated. Also thank you Susie Miles for joining one of our writing retreats. She shared with us how she creates autobiographical presentations which inspired our writing styles. Thank you Vadio Jansky, of Vadio Rocks Graphic Design Studio in London, for offering your time and skills in designing our book cover.

Finally, thank you Amazon's Kindle Direct Publishing for making it straight-forward for authors with important messages to have a global platform to make a difference.

♡

Doug Dunn

End notes

[i] The principle of *non-refoulement* is the cornerstone of asylum and of international refugee law. Following from the right to seek and to enjoy in other countries asylum from persecution, as set forth in Article 14 of the Universal Declaration of Human Rights.

[ii] A five weekend course created by Landmark, www.landmarkworldwide.com

[iii] The Anglo-Indians by S. Muthiah and H Maclure, 2013.

[iv] BBC documentary Presenter DrJasmin Khan.

[v] Bhowani Junction, by John Masters, 1954.

[vi] The Jungle, by Joe Murphy and Joe Robertson, performed at the Young Vic in 2017.

[vii] Moon sculpture, installed by Luke Jerram, 2018.

[viii] Team Management and Leadership program. www.landmarkworldwide.com/advanced-programs/communication-programs

[ix] Mobile Money uses the mobile phone number as the account number allowing money to be transferred around the world safely and securely without the need for a bank account.

[x] UBUNTU. Contributionism – A Blueprint For Human Prosperity. Michael Tellinger, 2013.

[xi] See OneTaste for more information. https://onaste.us

Printed in Great Britain
by Amazon